NOT TO BE TRUSTED

BY

JESSICA AYRE

MILLS & BOON LIMITED
15–16 BROOK'S MEWS
LONDON W1A 1DR

First published 1982

© Jessica Ayre 1982

Australian copyright 1982

100444992

ISBN 0 263 10013 8

Set in Monophoto Baskerville 11 pt.
07/0282

Made and printed in Great Britain by
Richard Clay (The Chaucer Press) Ltd,
Bungay, Suffolk

CHAPTER ONE

'MEN,' Lynda heard her mother's tired voice saying, 'are not to be trusted.'

The words came back to her now as she felt herself being eyed appreciatively by the man next to her. She strode firmly out of the lift without looking back, swinging her large bag over her shoulder.

She had never discovered exactly what it was in her mother's life that had led this generally quiet, reticent woman to such an observation. But it had nonetheless become part of her legacy. Like her long legs and quick dark eyes. Perhaps it was only her mother's sense of being betrayed by her father's early death; being left alone with three young girls and a farm to run. She had run it, too, and in the process given the three of them a living example of the value of independence.

Lynda pushed open the office door, to be greeted by a blaze of sunlight. After two months here she was still thrilled every time she walked in. It was so unexpected, this vast light-filled space on the top floor of what had once been a dingy factory building. Very elegant too, now, with its girded glass roof, giant hanging plants proliferating everywhere and brightly coloured desks and chairs. She returned smiles and nods from all sides as she made her way to her corner.

Her corner. Just over three months ago she had sat with trembling hands and dry mouth while Mr Dunlop had paced in front of her explaining with stern gestures what would be required of her if Dunlop Associates were to take her on. It was a new departure for this architectural firm to have their own interior designer. But the younger architects in the group had thought it would facilitate certain projects and possibly attract clients who wanted the extra service. It had to be someone young, with fresh ideas, someone who could think up projects on her own as well as work within the group. Could she do it?

Lynda had swallowed hard. Mr Dunlop had stopped pacing to look her directly in the eyes.

'Above all,' he had said giving her an almost paternal once-over, 'will you be able to stand the pace?'

She had understood at once that he was referring to her inexperience. Was she going to be able to manage alone in a city like London? Trying hard to hide her own fear, she had stammered out what must have been a yes. And here she was now, in her own corner, with the rest of a year's trial contract still to go.

She cast a glance at the blue of the canal waters just visible from the window and at the greenery above her desk before perching on her high stool. More reassuring these sights than the memory of the prizes she had won at art school for work she now thought amateurish. Still, all those years of sketching to scale had helped, as did her colour sense. She looked down at the design she had begun yesterday, only to hear a 'Hello, Lynda,' at her side. It was Tricia, Mr Dunlop's secretary and her flatmate.

When Lynda had first got her job and was flat-hunting, Tricia had suggested she move in with her. She could use some help with the rent money. Lynda had accepted gratefully but with a little trepidation.

Tricia was the kind of woman she had thought existed only in fashion magazines: a coolly poised blonde who seemed to walk through rooms and men with equal ease. She rarely came home before the small hours of the morning, if at all, but still managed to be at her desk, efficiently bent over typewriter or file by nine a.m. So far things between them had gone quite smoothly, though Lynda always felt she wanted to vanish when Tricia tried to engage her in what she laughingly termed 'women's talk', which seemed to be mostly about men . . .

Now Tricia placed a file by Lynda's side and with a meaningful smile said, 'Orders are that you familiarise yourself with this. And quickly!'

Lynda took hold of the file, but before she had a chance to open it a deep voice rebounded from Mr Dunlop's room at the other end of the large open plan office.

'I won't have it! I simply will not allow this project to be thrown away.' The words were clearly audible, even at Lynda's distance, and they were followed by the slam of a heavy door.

'Oh-oh,' said Tricia. 'It's himself again. I'd better get back and see if I can soothe Mr Dunlop's nerves.'

'Himself' was of course Paul Overton. It hadn't taken Lynda long to discover that. He was Dunlop Associates' rising star, and though he seemed to spend less time in the office than the others, when he was there it didn't take more than thirty seconds for everyone to be aware of his presence. Not that he always created scenes; there was only one other that Lynda could remember. But he generated electricity. They all felt it. Even when he was having a quiet chat with some of the other architects, a hush of expectation would fall over the group. Lynda had observed him on occasion and had done her best to keep her distance. She didn't want those aloof steely blue eyes fixed on her or her work—both would wither.

Tricia, filling her in on office names and faces, had given her a picture of Paul Overton's meteoric rise. He had joined Dunlop Associates some three years back after working in France and the United States. Almost immediately he had won the firm a contract for a new Northern theatre. 'Won by competition,' Tricia stressed. 'Picture all over the papers.'

Overton had never looked back. He seemed to be as adept at private as public housing and his name was now one to be reckoned with. 'As for the rest,' Tricia put on her wry women's talk voice, 'I hear he's no slouch. But not a glance at any of us in the office. Believe me, I've done my best,' and she playfully crossed and uncrossed a smooth leg.

Lynda chuckled, picturing Tricia's mock seductive gesture, and then remembered the file she had been 'ordered' to look through quickly. *Stately Homes*, it was entitled. She read through the introductory pages.

Given increasing maintenance costs, it was becoming impossible to keep some of Britain's most beautiful houses—even with the aid of Government grants—in good repair. But if proper planning permission were obtained, and suitable backers, many of these homes could be turned into exquisite period hotels along the lines of the paradors in Spain.

Conversion and extension would vary from home to home, but in all cases the original houses and grounds would be kept intact. There followed pages of detail on the potential properties.

'Wonderful idea,' Lynda thought, then glanced at the back leaf to see who had initiated the project. Paul Overton's name was at the top of the list.

Suddenly she tensed. Without looking up she knew he was standing over her.

'Find the project interesting, Miss Harrow?' He emphasised the r's in her name, putting a space around it as if it were an odd name to settle on his tongue.

She turned to face him, meeting the steely deep-set eyes, the slightly sardonic turn of the mouth. 'He's deliberately trying to make me uncomfortable,' she thought to herself. She took a deep breath, re-membering to pace her words, and confronted him, coolly, she hoped.

'I've barely had time to take it in, but yes, it does seem interesting. Ambitious.' She added the word as an afterthought.

He looked at her curiously. 'Good. Good, Miss Harrow.' Again the space around her name. 'Take fifteen minutes to take it in, as you say, and then come and talk to Mr Dunlop and myself about it.'

'Yes, sir,' she muttered under her breath, noticing for the first time the width of his cheekbones, the lightness of his step as he moved away.

'Insufferable egotist!' she thought, glad that her colouring didn't allow too much of the warmth she felt to creep into her face. She buried herself in the papers, hoping that she could absorb at least a little of the detail.

Fifteen minutes later, she got up, smoothed her dark trousers, made sure her shirt was neatly tucked in and began to walk, file in hand, towards Mr Dunlop's office.

Ted, at the desk just next to hers gave her a warm smile and large wink. 'Courage, girl,' he stage-whis-pered, and she realised that Overton's visit to her corner must have been widely observed.

As she knocked at Mr Dunlop's door, it occurred

to her that Overton was the only person in the office who called her Miss Harrow. Another device to draw attention to his superiority. She steeled herself to the interview.

'Ah, Lynda. Come in, come in, sit down here,' Mr Dunlop's voice ushered her into his large tidy office and pointed her to a comfortable chair opposite Paul Overton's. He sat there, long legs stretched luxuriously in front of him and scarcely looked up as she walked in. 'Rude so-and-so!' she thought.

'Lynda, you know Paul Overton, of course, and you have some inkling of why we've called this interview?' Mr Dunlop's voice trailed off as he tried to ease the tension of the moment by lighting his habitual pipe.

'Yes. Well, no, not exactly,' Lynda tried to calm herself by focusing on Mr Dunlop alone. 'It's to do with the Stately Homes file?'

'Yes.' Mr Dunlop took several puffs at his pipe and concentrated his gaze just above her head. 'You probably realise that if the project comes through, it will be the biggest contract the group has taken on in years and it will keep us busy for some time to come.

'It's Paul's doing, of course,' he glanced quickly at the near-slouching figure at his side and cleared his throat. 'There are problems, innumerable ones which we're not here to discuss now. But one, and it's a significant one, does concern you.' Mr Dunlop glanced at Paul again, looking as if he hoped for some help.

'The clients are more or less willing to go ahead with two of the homes in question, but they want us to oversee the entire project from roofs and landscaping down to the last chair. The interior design work will be difficult and administratively complicated, not only because of the sheer number of details, but because everything must be right. In keeping with period flavour, you know.' He puffed at his pipe again, got up and began to pace.

'In all fairness to you, I should tell you that Paul doesn't think you're up to it. Too inexperienced . . . He feels we should contract the work out to an established design firm. I've been trying to convince him that you're here for exactly such projects. We would, of course, eventually get you some freelance help . . .' He paused for a long minute, waiting for Paul, who finally stirred himself into motion.

Casually he reached for his cigarettes—Gitanes, she noticed—lit one without offering them round, and tucked cigarettes and lighter into a tight trouser pocket. Then he fixed his eyes on her, giving her an insolent once-over.

'What Mr Dunlop has omitted to mention is that by using you, Miss Harrow, Dunlop Associates will be saving a not inconsequential sum. Whereas I do in fact have a vested interest in the project being done *well*.' On the last word, he put out his half-smoked cigarette and raised himself to his full height.

'I have nothing more to say. You can discuss the matter further between yourselves. The decision, finally and unfortunately, is not mine alone.' With that he strode out of the room.

Mr Dunlop cleared his throat again. 'Yes, well, I'm sorry about that, Lynda. Politeness is not always one of Paul's virtues. A little hot-blooded, in fact. But a fine architect. We're lucky to have him.' He looked at her firmly with a quiet smile.

'Paul is right, you know. The project has to be done well, very well. I have a hunch you can do it. But think it over tonight. Read through the material carefully, and let me know tomorrow whether you want to start on it. We have a little time to play with and if your initial drawings are wrong, there's still time to go elsewhere.' He ushered her out, looking for all the world as if he wanted to pat her on the shoulder.

Lynda hadn't walked more than a few steps before she found Tricia at her side.

'What's up? Has our star been having a go at you? You look as if you're about to burst in tears.'

'I am.' Lynda tried a wobbly grin.

'Come on, I'll buy you a drink.'

Lynda's feelings were in a jumble. She would have liked to steal away to some quiet corner and think things over. But it would be better to sit in a dark pub with Tricia than to meet all the questioning looks on the way back to her desk. So she tucked the file under her arm and allowed Tricia to steer her towards the lift.

Glancing out the window, Lynda noticed two dark barges in the canal. One carried a low crane and was shovelling heaps of black ooze out of the murky water. 'A dredging operation,' she thought with a sense of foreboding. 'Or they're looking for a body.'

'Stop it, Lynda!' Tricia's voice burst into her thought. 'You look as if you've seen your own corpse! You can't let one confrontation with Overton get you down. What happened, anyway?'

Lynda took a deep breath as they stepped outside and threw back her shoulders. She began to describe the interview to Tricia, and as she went on, encouraged by Tricia's smiles and groans, the funny side of it took shape for her. Stately homes, indeed, created by a man too uncouth to say hello and goodbye.

By the time they reached the Rose and Crown, the two girls were laughing gaily. They sought out a back table. As they sat down Lynda felt a pair of eyes on her, and looked up to a curt nod from Paul Overton. She returned it with equal brevity, managing not to stop in the midst of her sentence to Tricia.

'I'll get the drinks,' Tricia offered. 'He does seem to have it in for you, doesn't he?' Tricia walked confidently up to the bar and as she passed Paul Overton gave him a scathing look. 'Had a rough morning, then?' Lynda just heard her say.

'It's going to get rougher yet,' he threw at her. Then looking over her head as if he had recognised someone, he moved purposefully away.

'Charming, just charming,' Tricia murmured as she put two glasses of white wine on the table. They both turned to see Paul Overton being lavishly embraced by a striking redhead near the front of the pub. 'One of his theatrical ladies,' Tricia announced.

Lynda excused herself. In the newly-painted ladies' room, she dashed cold water over her face and combed her thick dark hair vigorously. With each stroke she defied the face in the mirror. 'I can do it. I can do it!' And she fingered the fine golden chain which held a small locket at its base.

Pale but refreshed, she returned to her table, to find it flowing over with people—faces that she dimly recognised but couldn't quite place.

'Meet some friends,' Tricia welcomed her. She introduced Lynda round the table, but Lynda only managed to register the name of the man on her left, Robert Sylvester.

He confronted her. 'You don't recognise me, do you? I saw you in the lift just a few hours back. In fact, I see you quite often, usually striding off in the other direction.' He gave her a humorous look. She warmed to his generous face and twinkling eyes.

'Off in your own little dream world, aren't you?'

Lynda returned his smile. 'I guess I've been concentrating on work.'

Robert Sylvester, it turned out, was the production manager of the publishing firm opposite Dunlop Associates. He was a big burly man with a warm engaging face and loose gestures which suggested open spaces. Lynda immediately felt comfortable with him.

'You're not a Londoner?' she ventured.

'How did you guess, girl? Thought I'd buried my roots.' Robert delivered this in the thickest brogue she had ever heard. Lynda laughed.

'It must be my infallible instinct!'

They chatted about this and that, about Robert's job, his home north of Aberdeen which he had left at the age of seventeen to come to London. Then Lynda glanced at her watch.

'I must get back,' she said, the memory of the ordeal awaiting her clouding her face.

'What about dinner tonight?' Robert asked.

Before Lynda could answer she felt a looming presence near her.

'Enjoying yourself, Miss Harrow?' Paul Overton's deep voice was tinged with anger. 'You might just make sure that some of that liquid enjoyment doesn't spill over on our stately homes.' He let his eyes rest momentarily on the file which lay near her on the table, nodded at the group and turned abruptly away.

Robert let out a low whistle. 'Not in the best of moods, the mighty Overton.' He glanced at her curiously. 'Are you working together?'

She forced a wan smile to hide her humiliation and moved to go. 'Hardly seems so.'

'What about dinner, then?'

'Not tonight.' Lynda's mind was already elsewhere. 'I must work.' She took the file from the table, grimaced and tried to walk casually away.

When she came home that evening, Lynda wanted nothing more than to stretch out in a hot bath. She had spent the afternoon burrowed into the Stately Homes file. Paul Overton was obviously not in the office and she was able to focus on the work at hand. She began to dream the interiors, visualising how colours could blend in spacious halls. And as her imagination took free rein, she began to feel more certain of her ability to undertake the project. She made copious notes and began on some rough sketches, letting her hand do the thinking. Her first pause to look round showed her it must already be late. The office was almost empty.

Now she relaxed into her bath, grateful for its warmth, for the emptiness of the flat, for the soothing tones from her small radio. As she dried herself with her large maroon towel, her hand met the locket round her neck.

She opened it and looked at the picture inside—a strong face with its direct gaze. Her mother would want her to say yes to the project. 'Never let yourself be bullied,' she would have muttered. Poor dear Mother!

Lynda's mother had died the preceding year, without knowing about, or at least without showing the extent of her illness. She had been composed to the end, overseeing all the work on the farm, charting milk production, tending to the house. Lynda had not been with her at the last. It had all happened so suddenly and by the time her sister had reached her at art school, it was all over.

Lynda regretted this. She would have liked to have asked her mother certain things: about their father who was never mentioned since his death, about the source of her mother's continuing strength.

She looked away from the picture. No good musing now. She must have some food—she suddenly realised she hadn't eaten all day—and get to the drawing board. She pulled a pair of old, freshly washed jeans over her slender hips, put on an equally dated floppy sweater and walked into Tricia's tiny but tidy kitchen. An omelette would do, and some ham, perhaps.

As she beat the eggs, the memory of Paul Overton's chilling 'Miss Harrow' came back to her, his insistence on the project being done *well*, and she shivered a little. Perhaps she wasn't up to it. It would be far easier to say no now, disappointing Mr Dunlop a little, perhaps. Better that, though, than to have to live through the embarrassment of Paul Overton's contempt.

But no, she wouldn't allow herself to be bullied. She swallowed her food hastily and went to her desk, closing the door of her room behind her. Tricia knew this to be a signal that she didn't want to be disturbed.

The telephone startled her out of her Georgian setting. She rushed automatically to answer it, but then slowed her pace, knowing it would be for Tricia in any case.

'Hello,' a man's voice drawled into the telephone. 'It's your friend from the lift. Can I buy you a quick drink?'

It took Lynda a second or two to realise it was for

her: Robert Sylvester.

'Forgotten me already?' he queried.

'No, no. I simply didn't recognise you. Don't think I can take the time off for a drink,' Lynda answered. 'By the way, how did you get my number?'

'Tricia's number,' he corrected her, and chuckled. 'Come on, I'll see you're safely tucked into bed at the requisite hour.'

'All right,' Lynda acquiesced. She wouldn't do much work now anyway and a little lighthearted banter would be all to the good. It would clear her mind for the morning.

Robert appeared in under ten minutes. Lynda had just had time to pull on a slightly less tatty sweater and a pair of boots.

'I live just a few streets away,' he explained.

It occurred to her that he hadn't even asked her for the address. 'You know this place well?' she queried.

He laughed a little oddly. 'Tricia's an old friend.' Something in the way he said it made Lynda pull back a little.

I only ever seem to inherit hand-me-downs, she thought, and then wondered at the speed with which she had coupled herself with Robert.

But his easy manner reassured her.

'I think I'll treat you to a place country girls never see,' he said as he slid into the seat of a sleek new car. They raced along until Lydia quite lost herself in the maze of turns and narrow streets.

'Here we are. I think you'll enjoy this.' Robert ushered her down a few stairs and with a mock bow opened the door for her. She looked into a large softly-lit room with what seemed innumerable intimate alcoves.

A bar stretched along one entire length. Bright

posters and photographs littered the walls and mirrors discreetly placed between them reflected passing faces. Behind the hum of voices she could make out the sound of a sultry blues.

The place seemed entirely filled with people, some sitting at tables with chequered cloths, others lounging at the bar or perched on high stools. Catching a glimpse of herself in a mirror, Lynda suddenly grew aware of how plainly she was dressed in comparison to the elegant or outlandish women who dotted the room.

Robert must have sensed her thought, for he whispered in her ear, 'You look lovely,' as he guided her towards a miraculously free table. She noticed that people greeted him from various quarters.

'You seem to know a great many people here?' she queried when they sat down.

'It's my club,' he explained. 'Mostly journalists, writers, some publishers and theatre people. Food's good too. Would you like some?'

Lynda declined. 'A drink, though, a single drink,' she emphasised, 'would be nice.' She settled back into the comfortable chair.

'Tell me about yourself, then, Miss Lynda Harrow.' Robert put his elbows solidly on the table and looked her in the eyes.

She demurred, 'Not much to tell.'

But he drew her out and soon Lynda was happily recounting childhood escapades, her nights in the tree house; the death of her favourite cow; her early passion for sketching.

'You're especially lovely when you smile,' Robert interrupted her, and she thanked him with a warm one. Then over his head she noticed a familiar face coming towards them.

'Oh no!' she exclaimed, her smile fading. 'Look

who's here!' She braced herself for the encounter.

'Hello, Robert,' said Paul Overton. 'Good evening, Miss Harrow, I see you've wisely decided not to think over the project too hard. Or is it that you do your best work in crowded, dimly lit rooms?'

'Much like you, I imagine,' Lynda responded, surprised at her own audacity.

He gave her a quizzical look, then bade them both a pleasant evening.

'Small place, London,' Robert offered, to cheer her. 'Either that, or he's shadowing us. Do you think he's nurturing a hidden passion for you?'

Lynda couldn't quite bring a smile to her lips.

'Could we go now, Robert? Please. I have a feeling tomorrow is going to be a long day.'

She was hardly aware of the drive home. She only emerged from her reverie when she felt Robert's lips brushing her hair as she fumbled for her door key.

'Mmm,' he murmured, and gave her hand a large squeeze. Then in his best brogue, 'Lassies like you needn't worry too much about the Paul Overtons of this world.'

CHAPTER TWO

LYNDA woke the next morning with a sense of panic. She had been walking, then stumbling and running through dark corridors raw with the smell of vegetation, yet enclosed. One corridor led inexorably to another. The promise of an exit was never fulfilled and she knew she could not turn back. Behind her an unidentifiable presence loomed, gave chase. Just as it was about to pounce, she fell through an opening and awoke with an abrupt start.

She lay still for a moment, trying to wipe the bitter taste of fear from her mouth. An image of Paul Overton's disapproving face came clearly to her mind. There was something both austere and sensual in those wide eyes, those prominent cheekbones, the slant of the hard jaw. She shuddered a little and pulled the blankets up to her chin, trying to think sensible thoughts.

Yes, she would go to Mr Dunlop and put the case honestly to him. She wanted to work on the project, have a go at least. But it would be difficult if Paul Overton was watching her every step, criticising her at every turn, waiting for her to fail. Perhaps if she could have a week away from the office to work from home, do some necessary background research, it might be easier. Didn't Mr Dunlop agree?

The sound of Tricia grinding coffee beans stirred her from her planned scenario. It must be late. She washed and dressed hastily, choosing a simple green dress with a small white collar from her wardrobe. Tricia had said the dress made her look serious, studious, and she felt she needed that seriousness today.

As an afterthought, she pulled her thick glossy hair back into a low bun and pinned it loosely into place.

'There,' she thought, looking at herself quickly in the mirror. 'Couldn't look any more determinedly serious that that!'

Tricia handed her a cup of steaming coffee as she came into the kitchen and eyed her with interest.

'You were out late last night . . .' she led expectantly.

Lynda had quite forgotten her visit to Robert's club and she replied absently, 'Oh yes, Robert took me out for a drink.' She noticed Tricia stiffen slightly and look away with a just audible, 'Fast worker, that one!' Then she turned a forced smile on Lynda. 'Rather nice, isn't he?'

'Yes, very,' Lynda answered, unwilling to put her mind to the question of Robert or what seemed to be Tricia's surprising discomfiture when she had so much else to think of.

'We'd better get going,' Tricia suggested. 'It's getting late.'

Mr Dunlop accepted Lynda's proposition amicably. Her reasoning, he said, was sound, and he waved her off with an encouraging, 'I'm sure Paul will be convinced once he's seen your drawings. I'll arrange a meeting for next Monday.'

Lynda spent the rest of the day in the architectural library looking through books on stately homes. She decided to concentrate on the first two interiors: one a Georgian home, another a neo-Gothic castle. Her ability to range between tasteful opulence and theatrical grandeur should, she thought, impress the mighty Paul Overton. She went home satisfied that her ideas were beginning to take shape.

Checking for the post, she found a thick letter

addressed to her. She recognised the handwriting at
once—David, David Brewster. It occurred to her
that this was the first letter she'd had from him since
she had started on her new job.

She was filled with a warm glow and she rushed
up the stairs eager for news. David was her older
brother in everything but name. They had grown
up together on neighbouring farms, ridden together
over the dales, her hair streaming in the wind as she
urged her mare to catch up with his.

As children they had played elaborate pranks on
their respective families, conjured up visible ghosts,
dug up unburied ancient treasure. During the time
they were both away at college, they would meet in
holidays and recount their lives to each other in
breathless detail.

It was David who in those years taught her to
listen to music, who played endless records to her,
commenting on movements, tone, pitch, or simply
sat down at his old piano and improvised for her
while she sketched whatever was at hand.

Everyone had always assumed they would marry,
though she and David had never mentioned it between themselves. There had been tense moments in
recent years when, as they sat huddled together on
the sofa looking at a musical score, their fingers had
suddenly met. Or once when her horse had stumbled
and David had insisted on carrying her to the nearest
shelter, she had closed her eyes momentarily and felt
his strong arms grasp her with a new meaning. But
they had glossed over such moments with jokes or
stories about their college lives. Glossed over more
on her side then on his, she had to admit.

Then, in the brief meeting they had had just
before she had come to London, he had taken her
hand, looked at her solemnly and given her a long

warm kiss. It was like a promise. But he had said only, 'I'll write.'

David was the only man her mother had ever talked of with warm approval. He had been with her at the end and the knowledge of this assuaged Lynda's own remorse. On his return from agricultural college, David had begun to help her mother out with the farm as well as working with his own father. In her will Lynda's mother had specified that David should oversee the farm until such time as he and her own children had decided differently. The two of them had obviously talked the matter through before her death.

Lynda sat down on the sofa and pictured David, his sandy hair and sturdy body, his large hands bringing out delicate tones from the old piano as he furrowed his brow in concentration. If only he were sitting opposite her now and she could pour out her worries into his sympathetic ear!

She tore open the letter eagerly.

'Dearest Lynda,' he began as always, 'I imagine that in your conquest of London you haven't had much time to spare for thoughts of us.' He then regaled her with news about old Mr Grout, the local eccentric; Mrs Peabody in the village store; his recent passion for playing Liszt; the death of Brand, his favourite horse. There was only one personal note.

'I shall be coming to London soon. I hope you can make time for me.'

Of course she could make time for David. She was overcome with a longing for the ease she felt in his presence, their rambling conversations. Only a little pinprick of doubt disturbed her joy at the thought of his being here. How would Tricia respond to him? Or Paul Overton? She scolded herself for her own disloyalty. David was worth a hundred of them.

Lynda made herself some sandwiches and heated the remains of the morning coffee, allowing herself a few moments in which to bask in the memory of those long rides through forests, across fields. She could all but feel the soft rain on her cheeks; all but smell the fresh moist earth.

Tricia's small tidy kitchen with its gleaming appliances seemed coldly aseptic when she compared it with the clutter of the kitchen at home. The old deeply grooved refectory table piled high with jars of freshly made jam; the well worn curtains framing a view of gently rolling hills which she could look out on every time it was her turn to do the washing up.

'Stop it, Lynda,' she said out loud. She would drown under this wave of nostalgia if she allowed it to continue and find herself scuttling home, her tail between her legs. She quickly drank her coffee and munched sandwiches. She had set herself the evening task of looking through books on period furniture to prepare for tomorrow's drawing.

She worked assiduously for the next few days, going out only once for a trip to the furniture museum. She was rather pleased at her own efforts. She had prepared the Georgian lobby and dining room and she felt the pastel decorative hues she had chosen, the elegantly unobtrusive furnishings, struck just the right note of unceremonious good taste. On the third day, as she sat down to the drawing board, the telephone rang.

'Lynda Harrow?' She didn't quite recognise the voice, but the emphatic r's immediately signalled the caller's identity.

'Yes,' she tried to sound nonchalant.

'This is Paul Overton. Mr Dunlop told me you'd started on the project and I thought it might be useful for you to have a look at one of the homes. I'm going out there now.'

'Yes, it would be useful.' His quiet, polite tone threw her a little off balance. She had never heard it before.

'Good. I'll have to pick you up immediately—it's a little way out of London. Would fifteen minutes be all right?'

Lynda gave him the address. 'I'll wait downstairs,' she offered. 'See you then.'

She stilled her nervousness. No time to change really, but she brushed her hair, quickly applied some blusher and some pale lipstick and then pulled her new fox-grey cord jacket out of the wardrobe. With a little twinge of guilt she went into Tricia's room to give herself a hurried once-over in the full-length mirror. A slender image confronted her and looked at her unfamiliarly from dark eyes. Drab, she reflected with a sinking feeling, except for the gleaming dark hair. Nothing like the striking women in Robert's club. She noticed a silk fuchsia scarf lying on Tricia's chair and impulsively tied it round her neck. Yes, her blues and greys now took on a special allure. The effect was right.

She rushed down the stairs and opened the front door just as a bright expanse of car pulled up and Paul Overton's long lithe body sprang from the driver's seat. His elegantly cut suit accentuated the breadth of his shoulders. Under it, she could make out the texture of a deep blue silk shirt, like his eyes. A pleasant smile sat unexpectedly on his face.

'Good timing, Miss Harrow. I'm so glad you could make it.'

She turned her eyes away as he looked her up and down.

'I'm sorry, I didn't have time to change,' she

apologised, lying a little, trying to avert the possibility of criticism. He eyed her quizzically as she slid on to cushioned leather.

'Don't worry, Miss Harrow, there won't be any lords or ladies present. The house is quite empty at the moment.' He displayed a set of large keys and firmly shut her door.

His formal use of her name still rankled. I must do something about it, Lynda thought, *and* stop behaving like a skittish adolescent!

The car pulled smoothly away from the kerb. Not quite daring to turn towards him, Lynda stared straight ahead.

'You might, you know, Mr Overton, call me Lynda, like the others do.' She could tell by his sidelong glance that she had not achieved the lightness of tone she had aimed for.

'Yes, of course. Lyn-da, Lyn-da.' He said it twice as if trying to memorise it, and still her own name sounded strange to her ears.

'Well, Lyn-da, do tell me what you've been doing on the project. And do please call me Paul,' he added as an afterthought.

She tried hard not to suspect a patronising note in his voice and began at first clumsily and then with growing facility to describe her ideas. When she first thought to notice their whereabouts, they were already amidst rolling countryside. A soft late summer light immersed hills and trees in a golden haze.

'It's so beautiful!' Lynda heard herself exclaim involuntarily.

'Yes, and we're almost there.'

He swung the car through a break in what seemed an extensive stone wall and manoeuvred slowly along a drive banked by graceful willows. Through the trees Lynda could make out expanses of lush green occasionally broken by the deeper shade of clumps of rhododendrons and thickets.

Then suddenly, in the distance, she saw the house, and gasped despite herself. Paul stopped the car and they got out. In front of them, set at the top of a gently rounded hill, stood a superb Georgian house. Its columned façade gleamed white. The sun bounced off an entire section of glazed wall behind which she could make out what looked like miniature orange trees. At the base of the hill opposite, a graceful white wooden footbridge curved over a pool of unrippled water.

'It's exquisite,' she murmured.

Paul took her arm to lead her back to the car. She drew away abruptly, jarred by his touch. Then realising how foolish her response must seem, she mumbled, 'Sorry, you surprised me.'

He gave her a cool look from somewhere in the depths of his blue eyes, then reaching into his pocket pulled out a pack of cigarettes and offered her one. Lynda accepted, hoping her embarrassment would pass, took a long draw at the harsh tobacco and blew out the smoke—too quickly.

He smiled at her, warmly this time, and an unusual twinkle came into his eye. 'You don't smoke, do you?' He took the cigarette from her gently and put it out in the car's copious ashtray. 'Come, let's go closer.'

The drive took them round to the other side of the house, the front in fact. Close to, Lynda could see that the stucco was run down, windows and wood needed work. But the lines were clean, straight, and the wide wooden doors opened on to a beautifully proportioned hall with a vaulted ceiling pierced to give a circular gallery on the upper floor.

'Strange,' said Lynda, 'this is precisely the house I started drawings for.'

'That's lucky,' Paul commented matter-of-factly, and led her through the rooms, saying little, only occasionally drawing her attention to some special features. She felt a mounting joy as she walked round these rooms with their light airiness and their cunning variation of shapes.

What had once been the library, as she remembered from the plans, quite took her breath away. Its gently arched ceiling, screened apse and panelled walls still spoke of the gracious comfort of another epoch, as did the orangery with its glazed wall beckoning out to grass and trees.

Lynda wished she could simply sit for a few minutes and let the charm of the atmosphere invade her. Paul seemed to read her mind, for suddenly two chairs appeared from nowhere. She sat and mused for what must have been some time, only made aware that she had been alone by the sound of Paul's returning footsteps.

'Good, isn't it?' he commented.

She nodded, her eyes bright.

'If you can tear yourself away, I'll show you something which will make you laugh. I've done what I needed to do.'

He let her out through the French windows and she followed him down the hill towards the footbridge. It was only when they were a few yards away that she realised the whole thing was an optical illusion, a bit of landscape fantasy. The bridge had only one side. It was quite unusable.

'It's wonderful!' she laughed, and this time she let Paul take her arm as they trudged back up towards the house.

He began to talk animatedly about the history of

the place. The initial structure had been there since Jacobean times, but in 1749 the present building had been commissioned by a wealthy banker, John Ruys, later ennobled. Then additions had been made throughout the century—a final one, Paul pointed to an outlying wing, as late as 1840. Paul's features, now that he was wholly wrapped up in his saga, had taken on an expressive mobility, and Lynda wondered how she could have thought him cold, sardonic.

'Had enough?' he glanced at his watch. 'We could get some lunch. There's a rather good inn not far from here.'

He held the car door open for her as she took a final look round the grounds. It occurred to her that to turn this idyllic location into a commercial venture was something of a desecration, and she voiced her feelings.

'Better that than total disrepair. You're a dreamer,' Paul said brusquely, giving her a scathing look.

Lynda was startled by the sudden change of tone, rendered speechless. Not a word passed between them during the drive to the inn. She noticed that they were leaving the house by a different route, but the winding hedge-lined lanes now gave her no pleasure. She wished she hadn't spoken. Paul's icy distance made talk impossible and she dreaded having to face him over lunch.

The inn was a large rambling one nestling under luxurious shade trees. Inside a warren of rooms greeted them. Paul seemed to know the place well and led her to a cheerful dining room where they were ushered to a corner table overlooking a large flower-filled garden.

'They seem to know you here,' Lynda offered,

looking up at him as he took her jacket.

'Yes,' he answered absently. Then, 'Will you excuse me, I have to make a phone call.' She watched him move across the room with long strides, noticed too that others looked up as he passed. Her mother's refrain about men came back to her. Paul Overton was certainly not to be trusted. Those temperamental shifts in mood, that sudden iciness, boded no good.

She tried to relax into her chair and glanced at the menu. Almost as if he had read her thoughts and were bent on disproving them, Paul returned with a warm smile on his face.

'A drink? A bottle of wine, Miss Harrow?' The force of his blue eyes focused fully on her made her skin tingle. 'Lynda, I mean,' he smiled mischievously.

She looked up at him, defiant. 'I don't usually drink at lunchtime,' she said.

He chuckled. 'Perhaps you can make another exception today.' He gestured at the table. 'There are no files to worry about.'

Lynda was about to make an angry retort, but he put his hand over hers. 'I'm only teasing,' he mouthed the words softly.

She pulled her hand away, acutely aware of his touch which seemed to linger even after her hand was free. She lowered her eyes. No appropriate words came to her.

He cleared his throat and before she could determine whether he was mocking her or not, he said in an even, gracious tone, 'The food is good here, simple but good. I hope you're hungry. Would you like me to order for you?'

Lynda could only nod gratefully. She suddenly realised she was ravenous, having had nothing but a

cup of coffee that morning and some scraps of left-
overs the previous evening.

Paul called the buxom waitress over and chatted
with her quietly about the day's menu while she eyed
him adoringly. Lynda realised that his manner was
impeccable, that his charm could be devastating. But
only when he puts his mind to it, the swine, she
commented to herself, mustering her forces against
him.

The soup, when it came, was thick, creamy and
substantial, and Lynda felt her equanimity return.

'Will you join me in some white wine now?' Paul
asked as they waited for the next course.

She nodded, and when it arrived found herself
savouring its dry, nutty flavour.

'This is good.'

'Yes, one of my favourites.' Then, looking at her
curiously, he asked, 'Does that locket you always
finger have some special significance?'

Lynda was a little taken aback by his observation
and rapidly moved her hand away from her throat.
Then thinking better of it, she reached to remove
the locket, opening its delicate clasp to show him the
image within.

He looked at it reflectively for what seemed a long
time. 'Handsome woman,' he said. 'She has your
eyes.' He passed the locket back to her.

'My mother. She died last year.'

Lynda could feel the tears coming to her eyes and
she struggled to smile.

'I'm sorry,' he said gravely.

The food arrived to distract them, a veal casserole
smelling wonderfully of fresh herbs. Lynda dug into
it with relish and wanting to move the conversation
away from herself said, 'You seem to know this part
of the country very well.'

'Yes, my family, or rather my grandparents, used to live around here, quite some time ago now. I'm always happy to find an excuse to come back.' He watched her move the fork to her mouth and she swallowed with difficulty.

'Have you ever been to the United States?' he asked.

Lynda shook her head and Paul began to regale her with tales of the American countryside, its architectural curiosities. His eyes flashed and his droll expression brought to life vast glass domes and drive-in churches. By the time coffee arrived Lyna found herself enjoying his company thoroughly. Dangerous man, she thought. You never know whether he's going to breathe hot or cold.

'That wasn't so bad, was it, Miss Harrow?' he questioned her with a playful gleam in his eye as he helped her into her jacket.

'Not bad at all, Mr Overton,' Lynda managed this time. 'There was never any question of your conversational charms.'

He gave her shoulder a rough squeeze. She shook off his hand and without looking at him, slung her bag over her shoulder and marched out of the room. At the inn door, she stopped herself.

I'm behaving disgracefully, she thought. Paul caught up with her and eyed her oddly.

'Come on, we can make our escape back to London together.'

Talk was desultory in the large comfortable car. Lynda made an effort to reintroduce their former good humour, but it was gone. As he pulled up in front of her flat, she attempted a casual, 'Thank you, I did enjoy that. I'll bring the drawings in next week.'

'They'd better be good,' he muttered, giving

her a curt goodbye.

And so they will be, you insufferable bully, Lynda thought to herself as she unlocked the door.

With the splendid rooms of the house still in mind, she made immediately for her desk. Her hand was surprisingly sure as she began some more rough sketches.

By the next afternoon, she felt confident about the project. She was ready to embark on some final drawings when the telephone rang.

'Hello, beautiful, where have you been hiding yourself?'

She searched in her memory to place the voice.

'Forgotten me already? I'm the man who ogles you in the lift.'

She laughed. 'Hello, Robert. I've had the week off to work at home.'

'Do you think you can tear yourself away to come and have dinner with me tonight?'

'Yes, why not?'

'Good, I'll pick you up at eight.'

Lynda stopped working early to give herself time to dress. She liked Robert's company. He was easy to be with, made her feel comfortable. Not like the wretched Paul Overton, she added to herself. And it was nice to feel admired, unlike some insect pinned up for critical inspection.

She looked in her wardrobe and decided on what she considered her most sophisticated dress, a soft black garment with straight lines and a wide black belt which set off her slim waist.

Not bad, she thought as she examined herself in her dressing table mirror. She rummaged in her top drawer to find her favourite earrings, rarely worn.

The doorbell rang just as she heard Tricia's grandfather clock chime eight. Robert's punctuality pleased her, as did, though she hated to admit it, the long low whistle with which he greeted her.

'The country lass transformed!' he made a wide sweep with his arm as if presenting her to a music hall audience.

She laughed.

'Are you going to offer me a drink?'

'I'm afraid there's only a half bottle of white wine.' He followed her into the kitchen, his burliness making it seem even smaller. 'And not a terribly good white wine at that,' Lynda added, remembering the bottle she had shared with Paul Overton.

'Anything with you,' Robert continued in his mock theatrical tone and raised his glass to her in a grand gesture. They heard the door opening.

'Anyone home?' It was Tricia.

'In here,' Lynda replied.

Tricia stiffened visibly as she walked into the kitchen and saw the two of them.

'Entertaining, are you?' She gave Robert a hostile look.

'We're just going out to dinner.' Lynda offered Tricia a glass of wine.

'No, thanks,' Tricia replied abruptly, and as she walked away murmured meaningfully to Lynda, 'I'll talk to *you* later!'

'Don't think the lady approves of my presence,' Robert commented, trying to keep his tone humorous.

'What have you done to her?'

He shrugged his shoulders. 'It would take too long to explain. Besides, we have other things to talk about. Shall we go now?'

Lynda nodded. But a pall had fallen on the evening which not even the cheerful intimacy of the Italian restaurant to which Robert took her or his funny stories could altogether dispel.

In the car on the way back he asked, 'Would you like to come back to my place?'

Lynda glanced at her watch. It wasn't late. But then she remembered Tricia's hostility.

'I think I'd better get back to talk to Tricia.'

'Right.' He glanced at her quickly and then said in a low voice, 'But, Lynda, don't take everything she says at face value.'

His tone chilled her. 'Do you two share a dark and hidden past?' she tried to be humorous.

'It's not that.' Robert didn't rise to her attempted humour. 'It's just a misunderstanding which doesn't seem to have been cleared up, or at least, that's how I see it. But I'd better let Tricia tell you her side first.'

He pulled up in front of the house.

'I won't come up—might get my head bitten off!' He smiled at her a little sadly and reached for her hand. 'Too bad. All this has rather spoiled the evening, but I'd like to see you again soon.'

Lynda moved for the door before he could say any more. 'Yes, all right. And thanks.'

She climbed the stairs slowly, preparing herself for a confrontation with Tricia. Robert seemed generous, kind, but Lynda didn't think she was up to defending him. Nor did she particularly fancy a long evening of women's talk and revelations. Still, it would have to come.

She let herself in quietly, hoping on the off chance that Tricia might already be in bed. But no, there she was, curled up on the long modern sofa in front of the television. Even in repose, like this, Tricia looked like a starlet ready to be photographed and the long room with its carefully chosen arrangement of cane chairs, lacquered Chinese-red dining table, large plants and soft lights was an appropriate setting.

Robert must be mad to take me out rather than her, Lynda found herself thinking, just as Tricia, flinging a strand of silky blonde hair back over her shoulder, uttered a cool,

'You're back early?'

'Yes, I was tired. Would you like some coffee?' Lynda offered, to make up for her lame excuse.

Tricia followed her into the kitchen. 'Did Robert take you somewhere lavish?'

'Mmm. Food was good.'

'Robert's nice, isn't he?' Tricia said it laconically, but Lynda felt she was angling for something.

'Yes, very.' There was a silence between them which Lynda filled by grinding coffee beans and washing out mugs.

'Look, Lynda,' Tricia finally said, 'I'm sorry I growled at you before. It's just that—well, it's all over now, but I used to be potty about Robert. And then something went wrong.'

Lynda felt this was her cue. She should ask what, but she couldn't quite bring herself to it. 'I see,' was all she said.

'No, you don't,' Tricia snapped back, then caught herself. 'Oh, I'm sorry. Maybe I'm not ready to talk about it either.' She put her arm round Lynda's shoulder. 'It's not that I'm jealous—well, maybe just a little,' she smiled, and then abruptly frowned. 'It's simply that I can't quite bear to see him here, in this flat.' She took a large gulp of the scalding coffee. 'It brings back too much.'

Lynda warmed to her honesty. 'You know, Tricia, if you'd rather I didn't see Robert, I'll stop.' As she said it, she realised it wasn't just an empty gesture. She meant it.

Tricia gave her a long look. 'You would too, silly girl. But don't be too hasty. He's a splendid man,' she smiled a little wickedly, 'and I'll get over him . . . in time.'

CHAPTER THREE

LYNDA walked into the office on Monday morning with only momentary trepidation. Greetings of 'good to see you back' came from all sides, and the large portfolio of drawings which she clutched gave her a sense of well-being.

She had worked hard and she was on the whole pleased with what she had done. The trip to the country house had proved an inspiration. She really should show Paul Overton a little gratitude for that.

She remembered to look round for him, but he didn't seem to be at his desk. A little anxiety suddenly wormed its way into her mind. Perhaps he was already with Mr Dunlop, prejudicing him against her. But no, that was silly. And in any case, she felt confident that the work was good.

She sat down at her desk, placing the portfolio carefully at her side, and glanced at her watch. Still ten minutes to go. She rearranged some things and sharpened pencils to pass the time. Then promptly at ten, she knocked at Mr Dunlop's door.

'Come in,' Mr Dunlop's warm voice inspired ease.

She opened the door half expecting to see Paul, but no, there was only Mr Dunlop smiling at her kindly and asking her what kind of week she had had. With a confidence unusual to her, she told him she had worked well.

'Good, I'm pleased. I won't look at the work myself just yet. Paul Overton rang this morning to ask whether you wouldn't mind bringing the drawings straight over to his house—that's if you're not afraid of contagion! He's at home with what sounds like rather nasty 'flu.'

Lynda was a little taken aback. To go through the drawings with Paul on neutral territory was one thing, but to have to confront him in his own house was something else. She wanted to say no, she would wait for Paul to be back in the office. But one look at Mr Dunlop's face told her that that would be a mistake.

'Yes, yes, of course I'll go,' she mumbled.

'That's the spirit, Miss Harrow,' Mr Dunlop encouraged her. 'And it's a house worth seeing, you know.' He wrote the address down for her. 'Do take a taxi and charge it to expenses,' he added, and then looking her straight in the eyes, 'And stand up for yourself!'

Lynda left feeling slightly bewildered. This was not the scenario she had foreseen. I might as well enjoy it, though, she told herself defiantly. Riding in a London taxi still gave her a little girl's thrill. She hailed one, gave the driver Paul's central London address and settled back into the seat, garnering her energies for what might await her.

The taxi pulled up in front of a large fine house in one of London's most elegant squares. Lynda rang the bell a little nervously, bracing herself for Paul Overton's appearance. Instead, a stout middle-aged woman opened the door to her, welcoming her by name.

Lynda found herself being led through an ochre-coloured hall to a high-ceilinged drawing-room. Three matching windows, stretching almost the full height of the room, overlooked the green of the square. She looked round appreciatively at the mellowed parquet floors covered by a rich Chinese carpet, the marble fireplace framed by two large porcelain vases, the exotic Oriental wall hangings interspersed with modern prints and paintings.

The room was spacious, sparsely furnished, yet gave off a lived-in warmth. Paul's taste was obviously faultless. Lynda sat down in a tawny leather arm-chair, feeling slightly dwarfed by its size, and waited. Her nervousness returned as the minutes passed, a growing apprehension which made her temples begin to throb. She glanced at her watch and started to pace the room, stopping now and again to examine Paul Overton's prints.

'I'm sorry to have kept you waiting, Miss Harrow.' His voice when it came startled her.

Lynda whirled round to face him. Her mouth dropped as she took in his attire. For some reason she had not imagined Paul greeting her in pyjamas and deep green woollen dressing gown, hair more ruffled than ever and looking for all the world as if he had just crept out of some dark cave. He chuckled huskily at her surprise.

'I guess I should also apologise for my state of undress, but as Mr Dunlop may have told you, I've been in bed with 'flu.'

He coughed, a little too selfconsciously, Lynda thought. The dark circles under his bright eyes, the pallor of his skin suggested the after-effects of a late night debauch rather than 'flu. She chased the insidious thought from her mind.

'I've brought the drawings,' she said.

'Good, good. But won't you sit down and have some coffee first. I've asked Mrs Sparks to make a pot.'

Lynda sat down at one end of the sofa towards which he pointed her and watched as he bent to light a fire. His movements were sure and skilful. A dancing flame immediately leapt from the logs. He turned, caught her watching him and threw her a long glance through heavy lashes.

'It will take the chill out of the air,' he said, pausing over the word 'chill' and making it resonant with possibility. She cast her eyes down, searching her mind for some suitable comment.

'This is a lovely house,' she said, heartened by the sight of Mrs Sparks carrying a tray.

'Yes, it's at last beginning to feel like home. I've been here some three years now.'

Mrs Sparks deposited the tray on the coffee table and withdrew as Paul thanked her. He sat down next to Lynda and poured steaming coffee into porcelain mugs for them both, then relaxed into the depths of the sofa.

'That's better,' he said, gratefully draining his cup. He leaned towards her to offer a second cup and she found herself noticing the dark curly hair at his throat, the taut muscles of his neck. His fingers grazed her arm as he poured her more coffee and she flinched, almost upsetting her cup.

'Miss Harrow,' she could see the fever points above the pallor in his cheeks now, 'Lyn-da,' he stressed her name and there was anger in his voice. 'Would you stop behaving as if I were some monster about to attack you!' He paused, stretching back into the sofa. 'I'm a sick man and I'm feeling far too dreadful to make a pass even if you were Greta Garbo and encouraged it.' He gave her an ironical glance.

Lynda's stomach tensed painfully. She fought an impulse to flee. Instead she finished her coffee in a hurried gulp, and carefully placed the cup on the table. She tried to control the quiver in her voice.

'I'd better leave you to get well in peace, then,'

she said, standing up.

'Calm down, woman! You're here to show me some drawings, remember?' he growled. Lynda could feel the blood rising to her face and her ears tingling. She had completely forgotten the drawings. Now she glanced round the room, trying to hide her embarrassment. The portfolio stood balanced against a large mahogany bookcase and she was glad to be able to turn her back on Paul in order to fetch it.

He moved to clear the table and make some space. She didn't dare meet his eyes as she slowly unzipped the large black case. But just as she was about to place the drawings on the table, Mrs Sparks opened the door.

'Telephone for you from Paris, Mr Overton.'

Paul grimaced and glanced at his watch. He turned to her.

'This may take some time. Why don't you leave the drawings here and I'll ring you about them later, or perhaps simply see you tomorrow at the office.' He nodded a hurried goodbye before she could reply and brusquely left the room.

Mrs Sparks shook her head. 'He should be in bed, that man, not traipsing about!'

Lynda asked to be shown to the washroom before leaving. Still bemoaning Paul's refusal to be a model patient, Mrs Sparks led her along the corridor and up a few stairs. She opened a door and switched on a light to reveal a large bathroom with a sunken semi-circular tub. One entire wall was covered by a mirror which gave off a soft golden hue.

Lynda felt as if she had wandered on to the set of some Hollywood production. She washed her hands and flushed face with the fragrant creamy soap and as she dried herself noticed a long silken negligee reflected in the mirror. She wiped the reflection from

her mind and quickly left the room, feeling like a
trespasser on intimate territory.

'All right, dear?' Mrs Sparks looked at her with
some concern. 'You're not coming down with this
wretched 'flu as well?'

Lynda shook her head and managed a 'No, no,
I'm fine,' and what she hoped was a polite thank-
you. She was relieved to have the door of Paul
Overton's house close behind her and grateful for
the crisp freshness of the open air.

A walk, she decided, would do her good. She had
been cooped up far too much these last days. Striding
briskly through the square, she tried to erase the
memory of her humiliation. It was the way in which
Paul seemed to expect her to do the wrong thing
which made her so intensely uncomfortable. She
must try to behave in a more composed fashion next
time.

In any case, she reassured herself, the drawings
were good, and finally it was irrelevant how Paul
Overton made her feel. The mighty Paul Overton
with his arrogant ways and sunken bathtubs! She
smiled to herself as she imagined how Tricia would
respond to her description of her morning's outing.

But Tricia had her own news when she came in
that evening. She burst into the flat with un-
customary clamour, nearly shouting. Lynda rushed
out from the kitchen where she had been slicing
mushrooms for a Bolognese sauce, but her fear that
something terrible had happened was allayed when
she saw a wide smile on Tricia's face.

'Have you seen the evening paper?'

Lynda shook her head.

'Well, just have a look at this!'

Lynda put her knife down on the table and took
the paper from Tricia. A large photograph of Paul

Overton confronted her. He looked more rugged than she remembered him in life, his cheekbones and strong jaw more pronounced, his shoulders broader. He was embracing a strikingly attractive woman with a dimly familiar face framed by masses of hair. She was looking up at him with a seductive smile.

Lynda could feel herself blanch, but she made an effort to meet Tricia's smile with one of her own.

'Have you read the caption?'

Lynda read: 'Brilliant young architect, Paul Overton of Dunlop Associates, and ravishing musical comedy actress Vanessa Tarn, have been much seen together in and about London of late. A reliable source tells us that wedding bells are in the offing.'

Lynda glanced briefly at the rest of the diary entry and then handed the paper back to Tricia, whose eyes were sparkling with a humorous malice.

'Serves Mr High-and-Mighty right! That little vamp won't give him a moment's peace—she's had more men for breakfast than I've had toast. But maybe the brilliant young architect of Dunlop Associates can handle her. What do you think, Lynda? They do seem to have been together for some time now.'

Lynda averted her gaze from Tricia and looked down at the paper. 'Well, they make a handsome couple.' It was all she could think to say. A vision of Vanessa Tarn clothed in the silky negligee she had seen at Paul Overton's house had suddenly blotted out everything else. She chased the image away and it was immediately replaced by a picture of Paul tautly bent over the fire. Then, like the postcard sequences in a children's viewfinder, her mind clicked through the morning's images: the house, Paul Overton in his rough-woven dressing gown, Paul pouring coffee . . .

'I hope they're very happy together,' she said with an edge of bitterness that made Tricia look at her curiously.

Lynda forced a laugh. 'I'm getting to sound quite as nasty as you! Come on, let's get some dinner and I can tell you about my momentous visit to the Overton house.'

Lynda woke feeling refreshed and with a resolution on her lips. She would treat Paul Overton with absolutely cool professionalism. There was really no need for her to behave like a frightened little girl, and he was right, she had acted like one. After all, they were equals, working together on the same project. True, he was more experienced than she was, but she was learning, and undoubtedly she could learn from him.

Lynda fingered the locket round her neck, smiled, then got up briskly, washed and dressed with more care than usual. Stockings, high heels, a simple skirt of a richly autumnal rust and a matching sweater. She swept her hair back and tied it loosely at the nape of her neck with a yellow ribbon. Her small mirror smiled back at her. She would do.

Seeing the bright morning sunshine streaming through the window, she decided to walk to the office. The crisp morning air made her cheeks glow and her eyes sparkle. By the time she reached the office building and ran for the lift, she was ready to confront anything, anyone.

'Why, hello there, beautiful!' Lynda looked up to meet Robert staring at her appreciatively. 'My lucky day,' he continued, 'just the two of us in the lift.' And he grazed her cheek lightly with his lips.

Lynda gave him a wide smile.

'Don't!' he clutched his hands dramatically to his

chest. 'You'll break my heart!' Then as the lift stopped, he asked, 'How about wasting one of your busy evenings on me this week?'

'I might be able to manage just *one*,' Lynda bantered back.

'Saturday?'

'Fine.'

'Pick you up at seven. Perhaps I can arrange for some theatre tickets.' He gave her hand a parting squeeze and they walked off in opposite directions.

Lynda walked into the office and swiftly looked round. No, Paul wasn't there yet. She gave a small sigh of relief and hurried to her desk to prepare for an eleven o'clock meeting with a possible new client. It was a small job, but the kind she liked—a private house conversion. The family were to be away in California for a year and wanted the work carried out in their absence.

Her client was announced promptly at eleven and Lynda took him off into the small meeting space reserved for such occasions. They chatted about the kind of interior he wanted, the finances available. Lynda showed him a range of wallpapers, fabrics, floor coverings, and noted down specifications. Just as they were about to arrange a second meeting, the telephone rang. Lynda started. She realised it might be for her, but she had never had a call in the meeting room before. She excused herself and picked up the receiver.

The telephonist's voice queried, 'Miss Harrow? I have a call for you from Paul Overton.'

Lynda braced herself, remembering her morning's resolution.

'Lynda Harrow?' His voice sounded hoarse.

'Yes, Paul.' She made herself say his name.

'I'm still chained to the house. Can you come over

now to discuss these drawings?'

She demurred, 'I'm in the middle of a meeting.'

'Well, get it over with quickly. This is important.'

Lynda resented his peremptory tone, but she controlled herself and replied coolly,

'As soon as I can. Goodbye, Paul.' She hung up before he had a chance to say any more.

She deliberately paced her meeting with her client, making sure she wasn't hurrying things. Then, having ushered him out herself, she went to fetch her bag and tidy up before setting off. The Tube would do today. Let Paul stew a little. He should know better than to bully like that!

She covered the few blocks from the Tube station quickly enough, slowing herself as she crossed the square to catch her breath and collect her wits. Then, smoothing her hair, she pressed Paul Overton's large brass bell and waited for Mrs Sparks' cheerful face.

Instead Paul himself opened the door and loomed over her.

'Well, you *have* taken your time,' he said, scowling a little.

She rallied to it quietly, 'I came as quickly as I could.'

He was dressed today—a thick black polo-neck sweater and a pair of worn hip-hugging jeans. His face was pale under the taut brown skin and his eyes seemed even more deeply set. He stood back to let her in and as she brushed past him she could feel his pent-up rage enveloping her like a hostile cloud. She resolved again not to be cowed.

'This way,' he led her past the drawing-room up some stairs into a sunny open-plan kitchen-dining area. 'I'm just cooking up a quick lunch,' he said brusquely. 'Mrs Sparks doesn't come in on Tuesdays.'

Lynda sat down at the thick-topped solid pine table in the centre of which stood a large white bowl overflowing with purple and red anemones.

Paul said nothing, but moved round the kitchen with the efficiency of an old hand, whisking eggs, tossing them into a sizzling skillet, hurriedly chopping tomatoes and cucumbers, pulling out a large French loaf from the oven. He placed two brightly flowered Italian plates, cutlery and long-stemmed glasses on the table, uncorked a bottle of wine, quickly dressed the salad, and with a minimum of gestures placed the food on the table.

Her eyes slightly lowered, Lynda watched his every step. His fixed concentration seemed to have obliterated her presence. Then, having heaped her plate with the fluffy omelette and some salad, he sat down opposite her.

'I'm not very hungry,' she heard herself say from a long distance.

'You'll be even less hungry when we're through,' he met her gaze threateningly.

She sensed he was coiled to pounce and she could feel her mouth grow dry. She took a large gulp of the wine he had poured and then another.

'How did your meeting go?' He was making a visible effort to be polite, to control the edge of his anger.

'Fine,' she managed, and then feeling the wine coursing through her bloodstream, she grew brave. 'But that's obviously not what we're here to talk about, so let's get it over with.'

He seemed a little taken aback by her boldness and looked at her carefully before answering, 'Soon enough, Miss Lynda Harrow. Soon enough.' He speared a large piece of omelette, chewed it deliberately and swallowed it down with some wine. They glared at each other, eating in silence. After what seemed an eternity of chewing and swallowing, Lynda pushed her half-full plate away.

'I guess I should thank you for this altogether lovely lunch. Al-to-geth-er love-ly.' She was amazed at her own insolence.

He gave her an angry look and then draining his glass pushed back his chair and stood to his full height. Lynda followed suit.

I will not be bullied. I will not be bullied, she repeated over and over to herself as she followed him out of the kitchen, up a few stairs and into what was evidently his study. She allowed herself the brief luxury of a quick glance out of the tall window which looked out on a row of immaculate gardens. Then she tensed herself for what was to come. Scattered over a deep blue velvet divan, a thick-pile carpet of the same blue and along a long mahogany table were her drawings.

'Let's start here, Lynda, with the Georgian house.' He pointed to a watercolour drawing she had executed with particular affection of what were to be the entrance hall and lobby of the house.

'Yes, yes, it's beautifully drawn, beautifully coloured.' He made a large gesture round the room. 'They all are. Perhaps you should change your field and become an artist.' He said it with a slight sneer, and Lynda's stomach lurched.

'But have you thought of what these rooms are to be used for, their function? We're building hotels which have to stand up to a lot of wear and tear, not sugary nurseries and sentimental love chambers for the very rich.'

He took her round from drawing to drawing, pinpointing details, describing where people would walk, would sit, and as he talked his voice grew less angry, more patient. Lynda began to make mental notes of what he was saying. By the time they had looked at all the drawings, he was almost pleading with her.

'And Lynda, you must remember, we're working to a budget. We won't have museum pieces at our disposal, nor will you have time to scour the auction rooms. Try to take that into account.'

She needed to sit down, but there didn't seem to be an unfilled space in the entire room. Paul took in the pallor of her face and seeing her unsteadiness, cleared the divan of drawings.

Lynda sank down into it gratefully, feeling her head spin. Closing her eyes for a moment, she leaned back into the plush cushions. She felt rather than saw him come up to her and take her hand.

'I'm sorry, I'm sorry,' he murmured an apology. 'First I get you tipsy, then I lecture at you endlessly!'

She opened her eyes to see him leaning over her, his breath touching her hair. The rough wool of his pullover grazed her cheek. She wanted nothing more than to burst into tears and snuggle into his arms. But she drew away and made an effort to sit upright.

'No, no, you're right. Everything you say is right. I'm just too inexperienced. You were right in the first place.' She tried to stand up in order to avert her face from his, but he pulled her back down.

'Just sit here and relax for a minute. I'll get you some strong coffee.'

He left the room and Lynda leaned back into the cushions, kicking off her shoes and tucking her legs under her. She shut her eyes, but that only made her head spin more violently and she opened them just in time to see a large ball of burnished fur leap up beside her and purr with exaggerated ferocity. The cat walked round and round her lap, then settled himself with sensuous ease, demanding to be stroked. She obeyed willingly, taking comfort from the long thick fur, the arch of his back as his body shaped itself to her finger strokes.

Paul walked in with a tray and poured her a large glass of mineral water and some very black coffee. 'I see you've made friends with Boris, the lout.' He gave the cat a rough pat, his fingers just brushing hers as they met in fur, and then tapped him off her lap.

'Coffee first,' he said, handing her a cup. 'Then, drink all the water.'

Lynda sipped the hot liquid and met his gaze.

'I *am* sorry, you know. I didn't mean to be quite so scathing. But this project is particularly important to me. And you'll have noticed that I'm not the most patient of people.' He smiled engagingly.

Lynda couldn't quite return that. She emptied her coffee cup, making a face as the grounds met her tongue. 'It's all right—I'm just not up to it, that's all. You'd better tell Mr Dunlop and go to your established firm.'

He looked at her hard. 'I didn't say that's what I wanted to do, did I?' He seemed to be about to lecture her again. 'As far as I'm concerned you can have another go. This isn't a college, you know. It's a tough racket and you have to be able to take criticism.' He caught himself at his own sententiousness and smiled. 'Well, sleep on it, anyhow. I'll give you a ring tomorrow.'

Lynda pulled on her shoes and got up to leave, feeling herself dismissed.

'I'll get you a taxi,' Paul offered.

She shook her head. 'The air will do me good.'

He moved to gather her drawings, but she shook her head again.

Paul shrugged his shoulders and saw her to the door. 'Sleep on it, remember?'

Lynda raced down the stairs, almost colliding with a tall redhead who had just emerged from a white sports car. They eyed each other briefly and Lynda dashed off, hair streaming out from the yellow ribbon, tears once again rushing to her eyes. She slowed her pace when she reached the other end of the square and took a deep breath. Then she walked randomly, not quite sure of her bearings. Finally she hailed a taxi and gave her home address. There was no point in going back to the office in this state. The only thing she wanted now was to be alone in her room, to cry silently into her pillow.

That was how Tricia found her when she came in after work that evening—fully clothed, sprawled out on her bed, head buried in a soggy pillow from which muffled sobbing emerged.

'What is it, Lynda? What's happened?'

Lynda raised a tear-stained face and tried a quivering smile.

'It's all right. I'm just being silly,' but the tears continued to pour down.

Tricia searched Lynda's face. 'Is it bad news from home? Or is it the ogre who's done this to you?'

Lynda couldn't bring herself to answer.

'Wait a minute, I'll get you something to make you feel better.'

Tricia went out of the room, only to come back almost instantly with a large glass of brandy and a cool moist face cloth. She raised Lynda's head and made her drink, then wiped her face with the cloth. She waited for Lynda to compose herself. Then she asked, 'Do you want to talk about it?'

Lynda shrugged her shoulders. 'There isn't much to say. Paul Overton thinks the work on the project isn't good enough. And the trouble is, he's right. I think I'm suffering from wounded vanity.' She managed a crooked smile.

'Was he foul to you?'

Lynda grimaced. 'A little.' But then the sensation of Paul's breath in her hair came back to her. 'No, not really. Finally he was kind,' she swallowed hard as she said it.

Tricia raised her eyebrows. 'Kind? I find that hard to believe. Look at you!'

'I'm all right now. I just don't know whether I should begin on all that work again or give up.' She looked up at Tricia. 'He *is* a perfectionist, isn't he?'

'So they all say. You wouldn't think he'd have time to be with that Vanessa of his.'

Lynda stilled an involuntary shudder. 'No, you wouldn't,' she said bitterly, gazing down at her hands. Then she got up a little shakily, realising that the brandy had gone straight to her head.

'I'll fix some dinner, shall I?' Tricia offered.

Lynda nodded her thanks and sat down in front of the telly. On the coffee table yesterday's paper lay open, vaunting the image of Paul Overton and Vanessa. On an impulse, Lynda crumpled it up and walked across the room to throw it in the waste bin.

'There,' she thought. 'That's that,' and she switched on the television with unaccustomed aggression, making herself focus so rigorously on the image that the sound of Tricia's voice startled her.

'Lynda, it's the telephone for you. Didn't you hear it?' Lynda shook her head. 'Not someone I recognise,' Tricia gave her a knowing glance. 'Another admirer, I suspect.'

Lynda didn't immediately recognise the voice at the other end of the line, but when she did, her words tripped out and tumbled over each other.

'David, it's been so long since I heard you! Where are you? Are you in London? When can I see you?'

'No,' she could hear him chuckle at her eagerness, 'I'm at home. But I'll be in London next weekend.'

She pushed away her momentary disappointment. How wonderful it would have been to see David right now, feel his solid strength, talk about her fears . . .

'Will you stay at the flat? We can put you up on the sofa.'

David paused. 'I thought it might be better if I stayed with an old friend. I don't want to put you out.'

'You wouldn't be. But we'll talk about it when you arrive. How is everyone?' They exchanged a few more words and Lynda came away from the telephone beaming.

'Well, who was *that*? You look a new woman!'

Lynda laughed happily. 'My dearest and oldest friend.' As she said it, the truth of the words came home to her.

Tricia placed two bowls and a plateful of gingery fried pork and Chinese vegetables on the table. In between large spoonfuls of food Lynda found herself talking rapidly and delightedly about David, the many moments they had shared. 'You'll love him, Tricia,' she said finally.

'I'd love any man who could raise that kind of enthusiasm from me,' Tricia chuckled. 'Why have you been keeping him hidden for so long?'

'Oh, it's not like that,' Lynda suddenly caught Tricia's sense. 'Not like that at all.'

'Are you quite sure?' Tricia asked with her worldly woman look.

Was she? Lynda thought of David's warmth, the comfort of his presence, and she was filled with a longing to be with him. But she avoided Tricia's gaze and stood up.

'That was delicious thanks. I'll do the dishes and clear up. And thanks. For everything . . .'

'Are you sure you're all right now?'

Lynda nodded.

'I'm supposed to be going out for a drink with . . .' Tricia paused, 'Robert. We're going to clear up our misunderstandings,' she added quickly.

'Oh, I am pleased, Tricia,' Lynda said. But the pang that went through her made her not altogether sure she was.

'I just hope I come *back* pleased,' Tricia said wryly, as she swung her jacket over her shoulders and walked out the door.

CHAPTER FOUR

FOR the next few days Lynda kept a low profile. She went into the office obediently, got on with small jobs and avoided seeing Mr Dunlop or thinking about the stately homes project. Paul neither came into the office nor rang. She guessed he was waiting for her to make up her mind, but she felt drained, unable to confront the issue, as if she hoped some external circumstance would resolve it for her once and for all.

Then on Friday morning, Paul's voice came on the telephone. There was no preliminary greeting, no identification, simply a curt, 'I gather you've given up.'

His anger held a bitter edge of contempt. It made her blood rise and without thinking, she answered coolly, 'What makes you think that?'

There was a tense silence in which she could feel the receiver growing hot in her hand. She had a fleeting image of Paul flinging a well-stuffed cushion across his study, and she held back a nervous giggle.

'Miss Harrow, will you kindly stop playing around. This is not a game.' The controlled rage in his voice made him enunciate with slow distinctness. Each word seemed to bear a veiled threat.

Lynda countered it. 'You did, I believe, say you would contact *me*. I didn't want to intrude on you in your illness.' She paused, as surprised at her own audacity as he was, or so his silence seemed to convey.

'Paul?' she stilled the tremor in her voice as she

said his name, softly now. 'I will do it—at least, I'll have another go. If you still want me to, that is . . .'

She waited for reassurance. None came, only a gruff, 'Right, then. We start tomorrow. One of our clients wants to meet the designer on the project. It means a day with him in his country home. And bring a change of clothes—there's a party in the evening. I'll pick you up at ten.'

He rang off without waiting for a reply.

For a moment, Lynda felt herself reeling under the impact. Now she was in for it! How would she face Paul, let alone a wealthy client, for a full day? She got up a little shakily. She had to move, somehow rid herself of the cloud of anxiety she could feel descending.

It was too early for lunch, so she walked unsteadily towards the ladies, splashed cold water on her face and gazed at herself sternly in the mirror. 'Lynda Harrow,' she pronounced to herself in Paul's voice, 'stop playing games and get to work.'

She made herself smile confidently, marched back to her desk and took out the stately homes folder. As she opened it, every word of criticism Paul had uttered about her drawings came back to her mind. She took a deep breath. Here I go, she said encouragingly to herself.

On Saturday morning Lynda woke early and with a sense of bubbling excitement. She bathed and washed her hair quickly, smiling as she reflected on her own gleeful energy.

'Little country girl's big day out,' David would have said with a touch of wicked irony in his voice.

And she replied to his image, 'Well, I might as well make the best of it. It may never happen again.'

She brushed her long thick hair dry until it shone with an inner brilliance. For once, her reflection in the small mirror pleased her. The large eyes were full of a liquid sparkle, the skin glowed with health. She applied a touch of gloss to her lips, and, to celebrate the specialness of the occasion, some mascara to her long curly lashes.

Only when she looked through her wardrobe did she feel a momentary anxiety. What on earth should she wear, let alone bring with her for the evening's party? She rummaged through her clothes, finally pulling on a pair of grey trousers and a silky white shirt which brought out the rich dark texture of her hair. With her cord jacket, it would have to do.

As she took her best black dress out of the wardrobe, she suddenly remembered that she had been meant to go out with Robert that evening. The dress had reminded her. Oh, my God, Lynda thought, I'd better ring him quickly!

She moved to telephone, but just then the doorbell rang. She glanced at her watch. It was exactly ten o'clock. He *would* be punctual, Lynda grimaced. She smoothed her shirt and opened the door.

Paul's shoulders filled the doorway. Lynda looked up to meet his eyes and a shudder ran through her. His gaze seemed to fall on her remorselessly, and she turned away, covering her nervousness with a polite, 'Come in.'

'Am I too early?' he asked, echoing her politeness.

'No, no. But I'm afraid I'm not quite ready. Can you give me a minute?'

He nodded and she moved to write a note for Tricia. Tricia would have to make her apologies to Robert. The complications this might involve suddenly occurred to her, but there was little choice.

She couldn't face phoning Robert with Paul standing over her.

She glanced at him from under her lashes as she scrawled a few lines. He was wearing a beautifully cut tawny leather jacket which hugged his broad shoulders and fell loosely over his narrow hips and trim brown trousers. As he reached for his cigarettes, she could see a pullover striped in autumnal rusts and gold over a dark green shirt.

He caught her look and returned it with a cool appraisal that made her lose track of her thoughts. Then, taking a long puff of his cigarette, he got up casually, moving from object to object in the room. Each of his movements seemed to charge the air with a current, making the atmosphere so dense that there was no air left for her to breathe.

Lynda broke the silence, seeking to regain her composure. 'I still have to get a few things. Would you like some coffee while you wait? I won't be long.' Her voice sounded oddly muffled.

'No, thanks, I've already had too much,' and without asking, he followed her into the bedroom and watched her reach for her small overnight bag.

Lynda felt awkward, cramped by his looming presence in the small room. He sat down on her unmade bed and fingered the dress she had laid out. She felt it as a caress.

Lynda,' and he said it caressingly, gently, 'is this the dress you're taking?'

She nodded.

'Now, don't get huffy, but you know, it simply won't do.' He reached for her hand. She tried to draw it away, but his grasp was too firm and he pulled her towards the bed, making her sit next to him. She trembled slightly and forced herself to sit bolt upright. He let her hand drop, then with a sar-

donic gleam in his eyes, he stood up to his full
height.

'Miss Harrow,' he said in a mock-businesslike
tone, 'Dunlop Associates insists that its staff be
suitably attired for meeting prize clients.' He smiled
a wide pleasant smile that brought out the blue in
his eyes. 'We are now going to buy you a dress appropriate to impressing clients. Lechery should not
be discounted in these transactions.' He glanced at
his watch. 'We have half an hour to play with.'

Lynda didn't quite know whether she was embarrassed at his suggestion or relieved at his change of
tone. She simply allowed herself to be led.

Paul took her to a small boutique she had never
been to before. Its elegance frightened her somewhat.
He was completely at his ease and the shop assistants
treated him familiarly. Lynda glanced at him suspiciously as he moved towards a rack which held
several long dresses and deftly pulled out a creamy
silk concoction with simple lines and a deep cleft at
the bosom.

'Here, try that,' he said.

She obeyed, and as she pulled it over her shoulders
suddenly remembered. Vanessa, of course—he must
shop here with her. The thought brought back her
perspective of herself. Business, is it? Well, I'll show
him! Two can play at the impressing clients game.

She smoothed the dress and glanced at herself in
the mirror. It was perfect. How had he known? The
dress moulded the fulness of her bosom, fell grace-
fully over her hips, brought out the striking darkness
of her hair. She walked out of the dressing room to
confront him, and he eyed her critically.

'That'll do,' he said. 'Now try this and if it fits,
keep it on.' He passed a metallic blue jump-suit to
her.

Lynda tried it on, knowing that she would never have dared buy anything like this for herself. It made her feel like the heroine of a spy thriller. But the suit fitted perfectly, shimmering just a little as she moved, and she delighted in the slightly rakish air it gave her. She glanced at the price tag and groaned, 'A week's salary!' But she left it on, in keeping with orders, and emerged smiling from the dressing room.

'Good, good,' said Paul, looking her up and down. 'And it matches your jacket perfectly. Now for some evening shoes.'

The assistant brought over several pairs in her size and Lynda quickly selected a high-heeled slipper with an ankle-strap. Paul's cool gaze was beginning to make her feel like a piece of merchandise, and watching the composed set of his shoulders as he paid the bill, she grew increasingly irritated.

When the shop door had closed smoothly behind them, her eyes flashed.

'Do I get overtime seduction pay for wearing these?' she hurled at him.

He unlocked the car door and looked down at her angrily. 'Don't be silly, woman.' Then suddenly his tone was gentle. 'Relax, Lynda, will you?'

His gentleness filled her with remorse. As he manoeuvred the car through the busy streets, she said, 'I'll pay for the clothes, but it'll take me a while.'

'Just do your work well, Lynda, and that will be payment enough. It's a big contract.'

The word 'work' rang ambiguously in her ears. Was he referring to her drawings, or something else? She moved round uncomfortably in her seat.

Paul put a cassette into the car radio and the strains of Walton's Second Symphony enveloped her.

She sank deeply into the car cushions, stretching her legs luxuriously in front of her. It was one of her favourite pieces of dream music, and she let the ebb and flow of the instruments carry her where they would.

When she became aware of her surroundings once again, they were well into the countryside. She could hear Paul's voice as if from a great distance. 'Lynda, Lynda are you asleep?' He sounded irritated. 'I've been talking to you for a good five minutes, with no response!'

'I'm sorry,' she sat up abruptly.

'Well, we'll be there soon and I'd better prepare you a little. Do you want to stop and stretch your legs?'

She nodded, and after a few minutes he pulled off the main road into a small country lane. Then he mumbled almost under his breath, 'I can't quite resist this,' and drove along for a few more minutes until Lynda could see an old manor house nestled into the side of a gentle slope.

He stopped the car and they both got out. He pointed towards the house.

'I used to live there as a child.'

'It's idyllic,' Lynda breathed. 'You're very lucky.' She paused and turned towards him. 'Whom does it belong to now?'

He shrugged his shoulders grimly. 'Not to me, in any case.'

Lynda wasn't sure whether to pursue the topic, but she was curious now, suddenly realising she knew so little about him. 'When did you leave here?'

'When my father died. I was packed off to boarding school.' He spoke tersely as if not wishing to remember.

They walked a little more and Paul chuckled.

'Then a year later my dear dotty mum decided she was going to travel through Africa. She did, for six months, and ended up by giving all her money to various missionary centres. She came back to find that she had very little left except the house. She died a few years later. For the best, no doubt. The house went to pay off death duties. I was brought up by my grandparents mostly.' He stopped and stared wistfully into the distance, his eyes very blue in the clear light. 'Perhaps if the stately homes project comes off, I'll try to buy it back.'

Lynda wanted to ask a great many more questions, but now he quickened his pace.

'I'd better fill you in on Northrop Shaw. We should be there by now.'

As they drove the remaining miles, Paul briskly gave her details about their host. He was the acting chairman of the consortium interested in the project. It included two French, a British, an American and a German company, and Shaw himself was very keen. He needed little convincing except on small points. It was the American, Stanford Rees, who was the stumbling block and put up the greatest arguments about the scope of the project; was the most worried about budgeting. He might be there today too. Paul wasn't sure. Shaw was charming, and since his wife had left him some two years back, he was particularly susceptible to the charms of young women.

Paul gave Lynda a quick sidelong glance, as if once again checking on her suitability for the work ahead, and then pulled into the drive of a large grey stone house.

Lynda could feel her blood pressure rise. I'll show him! she said to herself, and opened the car door defiantly, flinging her hair back over her shoulders.

The large wooden door opened before they had a chance to knock and a butler ushered them in. A tall, elegant man came up behind him.

'Paul—we were beginning to despair of you. So glad you finally made it.' They shook hands and the man turned his grey eyes on Lynda and gave her a warm smile. 'And you must be Lynda Harrow. Welcome to Brecon House, Miss Harrow. We're very, very glad to have you with us.' He took her hand and gave it an unexpected squeeze. 'You probably want to freshen up. Williams here will show you to your room and bring your things up.'

Lynda followed Williams up a wide staircase and heard Northrop Shaw saying to Paul in a congratulatory tone, 'Charming, charming, old man. But then you always did have excellent taste . . .'

Northrop Shaw's manner was so pleasant that Lynda didn't allow his comment to rankle, and she quickly forgot everything as Williams showed her to her room. It was lovely. Blue and white ruffled curtains gave out on to a large garden surrounded by tall elms. A large, comfortable bed covered in white occupied much of the room and the pale blue walls were hung with watercolour landscapes. Williams opened a door for her and pointed to a small bathroom, then left her quietly.

Lynda poked her head out of the window and took a deep breath of the fresh country air. Then she readied herself. I'm going to enjoy this, she vowed to her metallic image in the mirror.

She walked down the stairs with a wide smile on her lips, letting the sound of voices guide her towards a large comfortable drawing room. Paul was standing in a corner, balancing a drink in one hand and a cigarette in the other. He was engaged in conversation with a striking, deeply tanned blonde whose enormous blue eyes fluttered intimacy every time she looked up at him.

So that's what he means by work, is it? Lynda grimaced to herself, then strode boldly towards Northrop Shaw.

'Ah, Miss Harrow, let me offer you a drink and introduce you round.' He took her arm and steered her towards the bar. As he poured her a generous gin and tonic, Lynda looked round the room and noted with approval the many small rugs, the tall plants, the way in which the armchairs and sofas were arranged to provide various small enclaves making the large room cosy.

'This is a lovely house, Mr Shaw.'

'Yes, it is nice. Paul provided my ex-wife with a wonderful designer. As I'm sure you are,' he added kindly, his eyes twinkling. Then taking her arm again he led her to a corner of the room where a man with a curly mass of salt and pepper hair and the most darkly intense eyes she had ever confronted rose to greet them.

'Miss Harrow, let me introduce one of my partners, Stanford Rees.'

Stanford Rees looked her up and down and offered a perfunctory smile, then sank back into his chair, motioning for her to join him.

Lynda sat down opposite him, acutely aware of his eyes on her as she leaned back in her chair.

'So you're Lynda Harrow,' he said in the deep mid-Atlantic tones she had only so far ever heard on radio.

She gave him a wide smile, watching his slow careful gestures as he lit his pipe, noting the casual cut of his tweed suit.

'Are you good?'

At first she didn't quite grasp his meaning. He

laughed, aware of her confusion.

'At your work, I mean,' he added sternly.

'Terribly,' she gave it an emphasis by meeting his eyes provocatively.

'As good as you look.' He focussed unnervingly on her legs, then bosom.

'Oh, far, far better,' she said with a flirtatious audacity which amazed her.

'Well, well, I think I'm going to like you, Lynda Harrow.' They got up as Williams announced lunch. Rees playfully stroked the silky fabric of her new jump suit. 'Mmmm, magic. It moves and talks,' he said, giving her a warm glance.

'Just like what's inside it, Mr Rees,' she countered, stepping ahead of him with a swish and almost colliding with Paul.

'I see the two of you have met,' he said brusquely. He took her arm with such force that she could feel her skin bruising. She tried to draw away, but instantly thought better of it as she noticed Stanford Rees eyeing them intently.

'Having a little trouble with your colleague, Overton?' he drawled the words, obviously enjoying their flavour. Then, moving away without waiting for a reply, he gave Lynda the benefit of a large conspiratorial wink.

'Insufferable prig!' she heard Paul mutter under his breath.

'Oh, I don't know, I rather like him.'

He scowled at her and dropped her arm. 'Don't forget we're here to work,' he said.

'I thought I was,' she replied softly, not sure that he had heard her now that they had entered a vast expanse of dining room echoing with voices.

A highly polished mahogany table took up almost the entire centre space. On it stood an enormous

bouquet of white and yellow chrysanthemums. Large
French windows opened on to the garden and at
one end of the room a long, narrow table replete
with attractively arranged buffet dishes was surrounded by the guests. She followed Paul towards
the table and heaped her plate with cold salmon,
tongue and a variety of salads.

'All right, Lynda?' Northrop Shaw was at her
side.

'Fine, thanks. It's a wonderful spread.'

'I thought you might want to meet Stanford Rees'
assistant.' Lynda followed him towards the table and
found herself facing the blue-eyed blonde she had
seen with Paul. 'Jessica North, Lynda Harrow.'

The two women sized each other up and since
Northrop Shaw had wandered off to make other introductions sat down together at the table. Williams
appeared from nowhere to fill their glasses with
chilled white wine.

'Are you from New York?' Lynda began ten-
tatively.

'No, the other end, San Francisco, though with
Stanford the travelling never stops.' Jessica smiled
her blue-eyed smile, just as Stanford Rees appeared
behind them and tapped her on the shoulder.

'I'm delighted to hear you talking about me, but
you really can't monopolise the only other beautiful
woman here. Move over, Jessica.'

Jessica dutifully moved one seat along. Next to her
Lynda could see Paul with an elegant older woman
in tow. She turned her full attention to Stanford
Rees, whose train of conversation startled her. She
had expected more flirtation, but instead he began:

'Overton is a brilliant architect. A little jumpy
personally,' he looked at her thoughtfully, 'but brilliant. Nonetheless, I'm not altogether convinced

about this project. Convince me, Miss Harrow.'

His forthrightness was endearing and Lynda did her best. He had a quick, ruthless intelligence and it wasn't altogether easy to reply to his questions. But the admiring looks he gave her from time to time helped, and by the time lunch was over Lynda was astounded at the depths her own enthusiasm had reached.

'Well, Miss Harrow,' he said as he pulled her chair out for her, 'you've gone some way towards convincing me. Far farther than any of the others . . . But that's enough shop talk now. What about a stroll around Northrop's magnificent grounds?'

'That would be lovely.' Lynda felt more than a little tipsy after all that wine and talk. She looked round to see if she could spot Paul, but he seemed to have disappeared.

As they reached the door, Northrop Shaw joined them.

'Can I offer you a tour of the gardens?' he queried. 'There will be plenty of coffee all afternoon in the drawing-room.'

Lynda nodded her reply and the three of them set off in the crisp autumnal air. The gardens were truly beautiful—well-tended flower beds, magnificent shrubbery and ancient trees, in the midst of which they came upon a strange clapboard summerhouse.

'My wife insisted on it,' Northrop Shaw explained. 'I think she had a fantasy of taking lovers here of a warm night,' he laughed a little hollowly.

Lynda suddenly felt a pang and caught herself thinking of Paul. How lovely it would have been to stroll through these gardens with him.

He noticed her faraway look. 'Tired, Miss Harrow?' he enquired politely. 'Perhaps a rest before dinner would do you good.'

'That's just what I need,' Lynda said gratefully, and bidding the two men goodbye, she walked towards the house.

In her room, she found her toiletries and clothes neatly arranged. She undressed and lay down on the bed, snuggling into its warm comfort. When she opened her eyes, dusk was falling, and she looked at her watch with momentary panic. Luckily it was only six o'clock. She relaxed for a moment. From next door she could just make out the sound of two voices, a man's and a woman's. The muted talk was interspersed with laughter and silences. She wondered vaguely who it might be; perhaps some late arrivals. Then she got up a little lazily and decided to run a bath. It would refresh her.

While the water poured into the tub, Lynda pinned her hair up and looked at her slender body in the long bathroom mirror. She spotted bruises on her arm. Fingerprints—Paul's. A chill ran through her from neck to toe and she drew her arms over the soft curve of her breasts. She could sense his rage as if he were standing beside her now. Lowering herself into the bubbly warmth of the bath, she protested inwardly. He has no right, and closed her eyes, luxuriating in the scented water.

Suddenly she heard a door opening, a door opposite the one she had used and which she had assumed was locked, and she looked up to see Paul standing there, ruggedly handsome in his green woollen robe, his eyes sparkling.

'Paul!' she exclaimed in astonishment, and drew a long smooth leg protectively up towards the curve of her stomach and bosom.

He said nothing, simply gazed at her as if his eyes were incapable of movement. Lynda felt her body burning. She wished she could disappear into the froth that surrounded her.

'Lynda!' Her name seemed to be strangled by his sharp intake of breath.

She found what she hoped was a reasonably normal voice. 'Paul, will you get out of here!'

But he didn't move, simply continued to gaze at her for what seemed an eternity. Finally he turned away with a grim set to his shoulders.

Lynda leapt out of the bath and dried herself quickly, refusing to let her mind dwell on what had occurred. An accident—it meant nothing. But the heat of his gaze continued to trouble her. And something else. If Paul had burst in on her now, that meant that the voices she had heard were his and another woman's. The thought turned her stomach. She fought to put it aside, forcing herself to concentrate on the business at hand.

She dressed slowly and with care. She pulled on the delicate bra and knickers she had brought with her and her sheerest tights. Then, standing in her new shoes, she applied more than her customary make-up, accentuating her dark eyes and full lips. Gently she pulled on the new dress, contemplating whether she should put her hair up. She decided against it, liking the feel of her hair against her bare arms. The mirror returned a complimentary reflection. Her brewing anger at Paul added a glow to her cheeks and a shine to her eyes. She felt ready to confront anyone, anything.

At the foot of the stairs she saw Stanford Rees.

'Breathtaking, Miss Harrow, breathtaking! Let me escort you in.'

Lynda smiled her thanks and took the arm he offered.

'My estimation of Overton rises by the second,' he said casually as they entered the softly-lit drawing-room. 'He's lucky to have you.'

She turned on him. 'He doesn't *have* me, Mr Rees. I merely work for him.'

A low whistle escaped from his teeth and he looked at her curiously. 'I wasn't suggesting . . . You are angry, aren't you?' He held her a little more closely. 'Good, good, I find myself drawn to angry women.'

He steered her towards the drinks table. Lynda noticed that the room was far more crowded than before. People seemed to have appeared from nowhere. She looked round, glad that Paul had provided her with a new dress. The women all seemed to be clothed in gowns one more sumptuous than the next. She clung a little more tightly to Stanford Rees' arm and held her head high.

As she turned away from the drinks table with an exotic cocktail in her hand, she saw Paul coming towards her. He looked devastating, his rugged colouring and dark hair set off by the gleaming white of his dinner jacket. His eyes smouldered and she lowered hers, seeking to escape before he could reach her. But he caught up with her and put a firm hand on her shoulder, forcing her to a standstill.

'Just a word, Lynda,' his hot breath scorched her hair. She turned round to face him, still keeping her eyes lowered. 'I only wanted to apologise properly. I didn't realise anyone was in there, let alone you. I'm sorry, truly sorry I was so rude.'

She raised her eyes to meet his and the frankness of his gaze brought a deeper flush to her cheeks.

'You look ravishing,' he said softly.

She turned away, unable to speak. This time he didn't follow her, and as she moved across the room she could see him being approached by the elegant woman who had sat next to him at lunch. She had a younger version of herself in tow, a girl of about eighteen, with eloquent grey eyes and ebony hair piled thickly on top of a fragile head. She was wearing a mere wisp of a black dress held up by two thin straps on delicate shoulders. Paul towered over her and Lynda could see from his look that he was drawn to her, focussing his full attention on her dramatic fragility.

Disgusting behaviour! Lynda said to herself, and suddenly found her clenched hands drawn to her locket. You were absolutely right, Mother. They're not to be trusted.

'Ah, Miss Harrow,' Northrop Shaw approached her, 'I've been looking for you. I was speaking to Paul earlier and I suggested that you both stay the night. It would be mad to drive back this evening— stop you from enjoying the fun.' He eyed her appreciatively. 'Paul said I should check with you.'

Lynda fumbled for words, suddenly terrified at the prospect of a night next door to Paul. 'But I haven't brought my things.'

'Oh, the maid will easily see to that. Do stay.'

Lynda realised that she couldn't refuse graciously, so she mumbled a faint, 'All right, thank you.'

Shaw led her into the dining room for dinner. The seating arrangement was formal now, the lights dim and Lynda found her name printed on an embossed place card. She sat down and was almost immediately joined by Stanford Rees on her right and a kindly gentleman who reminded her of Mr Dunlop on her left. At what seemed a great distance, at the other end of the table, she could see Paul beside the fragile beauty.

Stanford Rees turned to her. 'Shaw has always had a particular talent for seating arrangements, Miss Harrow. May I call you Lynda now that we're to enjoy a second feast together?' She nodded.

The food began to arrive and Lynda soon felt herself carried away by the festivity of it all—caviar on elegantly thin slices of dark bread served with flower-shaped radishes; pheasant roasted to a turn. As her various wine glasses were filled and downed, she lost track of the dishes in front of her and when Stanford Rees took her arm to lead her away from the table, she felt herself floating.

'Coffee? Brandy?'

'The first, please. If I have any more to drink I'll go straight to sleep!' Lynda laughed, and held tightly to his arm as he steered her towards the drawing-room, from which she could hear the sound of dance music. One corner of the room had been cleared to make space for dancing and in the dim light, Lynda could make out a few couples already on the floor. The large French windows had been opened on to a terrace lit with Chinese lanterns, and the cool air wafted in.

Stanford Rees led her to an armchair by the window, then disappeared for a moment, only to come back with two cups of coffee.

'Drink that down and then I'll give you a whirl on the dance floor.'

Lynda drank the hot liquid and closed her eyes for a moment. She felt Stanford Rees' cool tapering fingers on her shoulder.

'A dance, young lady?'

She followed him on to the floor and sank smoothly into the circle of his arm. He moved beautifully and she closed her eyes, allowing him to dictate her steps, then she opened them only to meet Paul's hot gaze. His eyes flickered at her briefly, then he returned his attention to his fragile beauty. His tall lithe form seemed to envelop hers and sweep her off the floor. Lynda stiffened perceptibly.

'Something wrong?' Stanford Rees whispered softly in her ear. She shook her head, but nonetheless he stopped dancing and led her through the door out on to a dark corner of the terrace. She shivered in the cool night air and he put his arm protectively round her, drawing her to him. Turning her face towards his, he gave her a long gentle kiss. She returned it, but after a moment he drew away, still gently.

'No good, young lady. You're stuck on him,' he drawled in his best American.

Lynda stiffened again. 'What do you mean? Who?'

'Our brilliant young architect.' He said it playfully.

She recoiled. 'What on earth are you talking about?'

He chuckled. 'Well, you may not know it, but I've been watching you and I do. I'm an old hand at watching women.'

Lynda's thoughts were in a jumble and she could feel her stomach clenching painfully.

'I think I'm tipsy. Perhaps I'd better go to bed.' She glanced at her watch. It was after midnight. 'It's been a long day,' she said apologetically.

'It's all right, Lynda,' Stanford Rees put his arm around her protectively, 'I'll see you back to your room safely.' He guided her through the crowded drawing-room and up the stairs. She kept her eyes lowered, not daring to look round.

At her door, he lifted her face to meet his gaze. 'You're a lovely lady, you know. And if you ever decide to chuck in the design side and concentrate on public relations, get in touch with me. The U.S. of A. isn't such a bad place.' He kissed her on the forehead.

When he turned away, Lynda let herself into her room and flopped gratefully on to the bed. Her ears rang with Stanford Rees' words. Could she be 'stuck on' Paul? Perish the thought!

She got up and pulled her dress off roughly, letting it lie in a heap on the dressing table chair. Then she splashed cold water on her face, barely patting it dry, and slipped into the cool silk nightdress which had been left on the bed. As she made to climb into it, she heard a knock at the door. Automatically she heard herself say, 'Come in,' and before she had a chance to counter the instruction, the door opened and Paul walked in, slamming the door brusquely behind him.

Lynda stepped back and covered herself with her arms.

'What do *you* want?' She steeled herself against him, uttering the words, coldly, distinctly.

'I didn't think you'd be alone,' he said huskily, almost apologetically. She could see the flush in his cheeks, his clenched fists, and felt herself irresistibly drawn by the sheer animal magnetism of his presence.

But she managed to reply in the same cold tone, 'What *did* you think?'

'I thought . . . Oh, Lynda!' He moved swiftly towards her, and one long stride was enough to bring them face to face. She stepped back, but he caught her in a rough embrace and crushed her to him. She could feel the tautness of his muscles, the rise and fall of his chest through his silk shirt as he moulded her body against his.

'Lynda, Lynda,' he murmured, burying his face in her hair. Then he covered her in kisses—eyes, nose, cheeks and with growing urgency her lips. She swooned in the circle of his arms, enveloped by his rugged odour, the rough wool on her bare arms. He was trembling as he lifted her on to the bed and pressed his hard body against hers.

Lynda felt a molten liquid rising through her, suffusing her limbs, her breasts with a scorching warmth. She raised her arms to stroke the silk of his shirt beneath his jacket, letting her hands trace the tensed muscles of his back.

Then suddenly, with an enormous effort of the will, she began to struggle, to resist him, to push him away. She jerked her face away from his lips, pounding him on the back with her fists. He drew away and rose to a sitting position, taking her hand in his, but she pulled it away.

'What is it, Lynda?' He looked into her eyes with a troubled warmth that almost melted her. But she forced herself to resist him.

'I'm not in the habit of going to bed with men whom I hardly know; men who are engaged to other women.' She said it slowly, letting each word take on its distinct weight.

His eyes reverted to the steely iciness she had known in the past. He stood up abruptly and looked down on her from his full height.

'And I'm not in the habit of pressing my attentions on women who believe what they read in gossip columns. Nor,' he emphasised it, 'do I habitually pursue women who lead on each and every comer.' With that he strode out of the room, banging the door behind him.

Lynda turned over on her stomach and felt the tears pouring out of her eyes. Afraid that he might hear her from the room next door, she muffled her sobs into her pillow, and only when the sky had lightened did she at last fall asleep.

CHAPTER FIVE

A LIGHT knock at the door a few hours later was enough to wake Lynda from her troubled sleep. She was immediately overcome by a sense of boundless humiliation. How could she have allowed herself to have been swayed even momentarily by Paul? The urgent warmth of his embrace came back to her, making her heart beat loudly. She closed her eyes in a half swoon, only to be roused by the repeated knocking. She stilled her quivering body.

'Who is it?'

'Williams, Miss Harrow. I've brought you some tea.'

Lynda crawled more deeply into the blankets. 'Come in.'

He placed a tray on the bedside table. 'Sorry to have to wake you, miss, but Mr Overton left instructions that you would be leaving early.'

She mumbled her thanks. Williams closed the door quietly behind him and she reached to pour herself a cup of the hot liquid. Her mouth felt dry and her head throbbed painfully.

As she drank the tea down a resolution formed itself in her mind. She would give her notice to Dunlop Associates tomorrow. Far better not to have to see Paul any more. The sound of a woman's laughter from the room next door strengthened her conviction. 'Treacherous rat,' she said out loud. 'We're all replaceable. A, B, C, or D will do.' She could feel herself convulsed by a pang of jealousy, a sharp stab which cut right through her. 'Treacherous rat,' she said again, almost wishing he would hear her. 'But at least I didn't succumb to your manifest charms,' she added to herself, not sure that her defiance wasn't tinged with regret.

Lynda dressed quickly in her own clothes and tossed the new garments carelessly into her bag, thinking she would do as well to leave them behind. She hoped Shaw was still asleep, that she could leave the house and get into the car unnoticed. There would only be Paul to confront on the drive back to London. After that she could put this whole ordeal behind her.

She tiptoed lightly down the stairs. At the bottom, she made out Paul's broad back. Her legs seemed to give out beneath her. She clung for support to the banister. Paul turned and seeing her came to take her bag. He made no sign of greeting, simply glanced at her with a hard glint in his eye. He looked haggard, the planes of his face more jagged than ever, dark circles under his eyes.

'I've said our goodbyes. Unless you want some breakfast, we can go now.'

She shook her head, relieved that she wouldn't have to face anyone.

They walked silently to the car, and Lynda braced herself for what she must make instantly clear. It would be easiest while he was driving; she wouldn't have to look at him that way.

As the car pulled on to the main road, Paul reached to switch on the radio. She stopped him.

'I'd just like to say something first——' She paused with the effort of removing the tears from her voice.

He didn't help her out.

'I'm going to submit my resignation tomorrow.' She waited for his response. He made none. 'I can't work under these conditions . . . in this situation . . . with you.' She stumbled over the words, searching for the right ones. Still he said nothing, and she glanced at him from the corner of her eyes. He looked pale, impassive, but his hands gripped the steering wheel with a rigour which brought blood to his knuckles.

Suddenly he swerved the car into a layby and jammed on the brakes. He turned to her, an angry scowl on his face.

'You are most certainly *not* going to resign now,' he said menacingly. She moved as far away from him as possible, frightened at his anger. 'Why, I listened to Rees for an hour last night, singing your praises. It seems you've convinced him that the project should be a large one. If you go now, he'll make one hell of a fuss.' He paused. 'I don't know what you did to him, whether he was talking out of sense or out of lust . . . though I can imagine,' he disrobed her coldly with his eyes. 'But now you're in, whether you like it or not. And whether I like it or not,' he added as an afterthought.

Lynda bridled at his imperious tone, at his iciness.

'I'm free to resign if I choose,' she said bitterly. 'You can find someone else to sell your wares.'

He gripped her arm with a savage strength and shook her hard. Then, all colour draining out of his face, he let go and made a visible effort at restraining his temper. His voice when it sounded again was husky.

'Lynda, will you please try to behave responsibly, professionally. This project could make your name. There'd be no lack of opportunities afterwards.' He paused. 'And it has nothing to do with what went on between us yesterday. If you like, I'll even attempt to apologise for that . . . though you did lead me on, you know.' There was a bitter edge to his voice and she began to protest. But he stopped her and said simply, gently, 'I am sorry.' She met his eyes and turned away, unable to bear their pressure.

He shrugged his shoulders and started the car. They drove back without exchanging another word, the music encasing their separate silences, until Paul pulled up in front of her door. He got out, opened the boot to take out her bag, then turned to her.

'Well?' There was an entreaty beneath his abruptness.

'Well, I'll do it—the drawings at least. But don't expect me to do any more of your dirty work!' She flung the words at him, simultaneously unzipped her bag and hurled dress and suit in his face. 'I won't be needing these any more.' And she rushed towards her door, leaving him standing there with a look of utter amazement on his face.

Lynda spent the afternoon in a stupor, dozing, pottering about the flat, not entirely aware of her movements or of the passage of time. She would find herself holding a dust-cloth, not remembering what she had meant to do with it. Nor was she aware of Tricia's absence until she heard a key turning in the lock. Then she mustered her attention and fixed a smile on her face. Tricia mustn't see her in this state; there would be too many questions to answer.

As Tricia walked in, Lynda offered a jaunty hello.

'Have a good time?' Tricia asked.

'Amazing.'

'Where did you go exactly?'

Lynda remembered that in her note to Tricia she had merely said that she was off with Paul for a day of work. So now she filled in, describing the house, Northrop Shaw, Stanford Rees, the sumptuous food.

She noticed that Tricia was only listening with half an ear.

'You look tired, Tricia,' she commented.

'I didn't get much sleep last night,' Tricia replied evasively. 'I think I'll go and lie down now, in fact.'

Relieved to be once more on her own, Lynda did not enquire further. She switched on the television, hoping that its stream of images would provide her with some distraction from the turmoil of her own thoughts. But there was no relief to be had from that quarter.

Her mind moved round and round the fact that Paul had used her, would have used her more had she not stopped him. And herself. Yet the sense of his body pressed heavily on hers was so acute that even the fleeting memory of it made her blood pound, her pulse throb so urgently that her vision was blurred.

She forced herself to focus on the television. Suddenly she recognised a half-familiar face. It was like an omen confirming her worst fears. There on the screen, gyrating silk-clad hips to the rhythm of a hard rock band, stood Vanessa Tarn. Microphone pressed close to ferociously red lips, she panted the single word, 'Desire, desire, desire . . .'

Then the music stopped and she bowed low to an invisible audience, letting her mass of electric curls sweep the floor.

Lynda sat transfixed. A cold hand seemed to be choking her, stopping her breath, paralysing her into immobility. She wanted to erase the image from the screen, but she couldn't move. Instead she watched. Watched Vanessa sink seductively into a low chair and turn luminous eyes up to the well-known television interviewer. Yes, she breathed throatily, that was one of the numbers from the new musical she was starring in. Yes, it was opening in the West End next week.

Lynda heard Tricia come up behind her.

'That vamp again! Don't know how an intelligent man like Paul Overton can stand for it. It makes me despair.'

Lynda didn't trust herself to reply.

'Come on, let's get some food before she cuts my appetite.' Tricia moved towards the kitchen and Lynda made herself turn the television off. Just as image and sound flickered away, she overheard the interviewer questioning Vanessa about her engagement to Paul Overton.

Lynda rushed blindly into the kitchen. Her hands trembled as she sliced some bread and cheese. Only the prolonged effort of chewing, of forcing herself to make comments to Tricia, began to still her nerves a little.

As she snuggled into her cool sheets that evening, Lynda resolved that she would put Paul out of her mind, finish the drawings quickly, and then look around for a new job.

Monday morning dawned grey and drizzly. Lynda wished that she could ring in to say that she would be working at home, but she had left her materials in the office. At the back of her mind, she realised, lay a desire to avoid Paul as much as possible. Still, it couldn't be helped today. She pulled on her old comfortable jeans and a warm sweater, and took her raincoat out of the wardrobe. Winter seemed to be closing in.

The office was almost empty when she arrived. There was no sign of Paul and she breathed a sigh of relief, settling easily into work. At about one o'clock she decided to pack up her materials and go off to a large fabric centre to do some costings. Tomorrow she could work from home. She left word with Tricia for Mr Dunlop and hurried off.

At the lift she bumped into Robert Sylvester.

'Well, well, well,' he gave her a friendly smile which belied his words, 'here comes the young beauty who stood me up and broke my heart!'

'I'm sorry, Robert, but Work called.' She flushed a little at the memory of what she had in fact been doing on Saturday evening.

When the lift doors had slid shut, Robert lifted her face up to his. 'You're looking pale, Lynda. Is anything wrong?' He sounded genuinely concerned, and the tears came rushing to her eyes.

He put his arms around her, drew her to him, patted her back gently and murmured comfort. Lynda relaxed into his solidity, burrowing her face into his shoulder. She looked up only when the lift doors had opened.

There stood Paul Overton. He eyed them grimly, taking in the scene, and then nodded curtly to Robert. As Lynda brushed past him, he muttered with seething contempt, 'I see you're up to your tricks again.'

She was too surprised to answer and rushed away blindly.

'Slow down!' Robert caught up to her. 'Would you like my shoulder to cry on? It's available—along with lunch.'

Lynda shook her head. 'I'm all right. And I have to get on with this.' She held up her folder and braved a smile.

'At least let me give you a ride.'

She demurred. 'The fabric centre I have to get to is a good half-hour away.'

'You really do want to be on your own, don't you?'

Lynda nodded.

'Right then, chin up, young lady. I'll give you a ring during the week to see how you are.'

Lynda smiled gratefully and walked off waving. At the corner of the street she jumped on to a number twenty-four bus just as it was pulling away. She went up the curving stairway and found a seat.

For the first time since she had been in London, the top of the double-decker didn't thrill her. The city looked dismal in the sombre light: tops of umbrellas, greying brick, blackened stone. She yearned suddenly for the rolling hills and copses of home, the deep greens of the countryside. She closed her eyes for a moment in order to see it all better, but instead the image of Paul loomed before her, Paul watching her with grim contempt written all over his face.

Lynda shuddered. Yes, she *had* been falling for him. And it was all impossible. Work aside, he was simply using her, or would—as he used any woman he met casually. Her face burned as she remembered how she had succumbed to his embrace as if she made a habit of such encounters. She had offered almost no resistance. It was too humiliating to think about. No wonder he eyed her with contempt!

If only she could erase the pressure of his arms, the touch of his lips, the imprint of his body on hers. She must get away—finish her work and get away.

Her hair streaming, Lynda entered the fabric centre, took out her notebook and began to make the rounds. Chintzes, velvets, William Morris prints decked the walls in a variety of colours. Gradually some of the enthusiasm she had expressed to Stanford Rees began to come back to her and by the time she got home later that day, she was ready to immerse herself in the project once again.

Lynda worked flat out that week, staying up late into the nights, emerging only for food and an occasional breath of air. There was a desperation to the way she drove herself, almost as if work was the only thing which could blank out her thoughts. Her nights were dreamless. She didn't bother to answer the telephone and she told Tricia to make any necessary excuses for her.

Finally, on Friday morning, looking through the drawings and plans she had completed, the snatches of chintz and velvet pinned to the corners, she breathed a deep sigh of relief. It was almost all done. She allowed herself the luxury of a long bath, letting the hot water take the strain out of her shoulders.

The telephone rang just as she had finished towelling herself dry and she decided to answer it. Paul's voice sounded at the other end.

'Lynda?'

Her first impulse was to hang up.

'Lynda, are you there?'

'Yes,' she answered at last, faintly.

'I was just wondering how the work was coming on?'

'Fine. I'm almost done.'

'Can I have a look?'

'I wasn't planning on coming in today.'

'I could come to you.'

He was obviously worried about her progress. She felt like letting him stew.

'It's not terribly convenient,' she began.

'I could come at any time.'

'All right then, if you insist.'

'May I come immediately?'

'Why not? We might as well get it over with.'

She rang off without saying goodbye, irritated at

his lack of confidence in her. Then she hurriedly put on her jeans and sweater, refusing to make a special effort, and went to brew some coffee. The doorbell rang before she had finished.

'He's really worried,' she thought to herself, and the idea of his discomfort brought a smile to her lips.

It disappeared as soon as she saw him. She had forgotten the sheer impact of his presence, the steely magnetism of his eyes, the mobile expressiveness of his mouth. They looked at each other for a moment in silence.

Then, by way of greeting, Paul said, 'You look worn out.'

'Hardly surprising,' Lynda replied with a hint of bitterness.

He raised a single eyebrow and muttered, 'I did try to warn you off initially, if you remember.'

'I remember only too well.' She turned on her heel, fetched the drawings and threw the whole pile down on the red lacquered table.

'Here!' She flung it at him, happy to see the flush of anger rising to his cheeks as she turned her back and went on with her coffee-making.

She sipped her coffee quietly, leaning on the kitchen counter and watching Paul covertly. His attention was wholly fixed on the drawings. That's all he cares about, she thought, a lump rising to her throat.

After what seemed an eternity, he got up and came towards the kitchen. She kept her eyes away from his, focused on her coffee cup as if it were the centre of the universe.

'Are you going to offer me some of that?' There was a hint of reproach in his voice.

She poured a cup and handed it to him, still keeping her eyes lowered. He raised her face with a finger, making her meet his eyes. She shivered at his touch and drew away, yet her eyes refused to do her bidding and stayed fixed to his. They looked at each other deeply for a long moment.

Then he said softly, a little hoarsely, 'They're good, you know. Very good. I'm sorry if I mistrusted you.'

Lynda could find nothing to say in return.

'If you feel up to it, we could just go over some small points.'

She nodded, unable to trust her voice, and followed him obediently towards the table.

'Now don't get upset. They're *small* points,' he emphasised it, 'but we want to get it right. They're mostly to do with lighting.'

They went through the drawings, one by one. Lynda's voice surfaced again and at one point she found herself arguing stubbornly for a particular chintz she had chosen which he thought impractical. By the time they had finished her eyes were shining.

'Right,' he said, 'only a few more drawings to do on the first two houses, then you can go on to the others. With Rees convinced, there should be little problem in swinging the whole lot.' He sounded jubilant.

Lynda faltered, 'I'll finish the first two houses, but I don't really want to go on with the others.'

'What!' He sounded incredulous. 'You can't be serious! I've just been telling you I want you in. How can you possibly go this far and not see the whole thing through?'

Lynda turned away from his mounting impatience and stared out of the window.

Paul got up and began to pace, searching for his cigarettes in his jacket pocket. From lowered lids she could see the varying emotions fighting for control of his face. Finally, he stubbed out his half-smoked cigarette and turned to her gently.

'Why, Lynda? It makes no sense. Why?'

She felt her throat growing tight and she longed to fling herself into his arms. But she kept her eyes lowered and simply said, 'Personal reasons.'

He exploded, 'Women! I don't believe it. What possible personal reasons could there be for giving this up?' His face suddenly darkened. 'You're not . . .' he fumbled, 'you're not pregnant?'

It was her turn to look incredulous. 'Certainly not! What do you think I am?' She pushed her chair back abruptly, gathered the drawings together in a heap and keeping her voice even, said, 'I think you'd better go now.'

Paul didn't move. He gazed at her steadily and after a moment said, 'I'm sorry—sorry if I insulted your intelligence. Look, can we go and have some lunch together and talk this over? You don't look as if you're about to offer me any,' he added, attempting humour.

She was about to refuse with a blunt, 'There's nothing to talk about,' when the telephone rang, and Lynda hurried to answer it, grateful for the interruption.

David's slow clear voice greeted her.

'Lynda, they told me at the office you were working from home. I'm not disturbing you, am I?'

'Of course not. Are you in London?'

'I've just arrived. Can I see you this evening?'

'Now, if you like,' she said it, realising she wanted to escape from Paul.

'Wonderful! How do I get to you?'

Lynda gave him instructions and came away from the telephone smiling. Paul looked at her with an angry scowl on his face. His eyes seemed to have turned jet black, his shoulders were tensed.

'So that's that, Miss Harrow,' he said scathingly. 'Perhaps I was right about you in the first place, after all.' He turned away swiftly and strode towards the door. 'Just bring all those drawings in next week,' he flung threateningly over his shoulder, and then slammed the door behind him.

Lynda quelled an impulse to run after him and say she would do anything, anything to please him. But what was the use? She sat down on the sofa to quiet her nerves. How abysmal to be so miserable just when she should be jubilant about Paul's praise of her work.

A knock at the door roused her from her thoughts. David. She hurried to let him in.

There he stood, looking larger than she remembered him, something of a stranger in a thick tweed jacket she didn't recognise. His face was fresh, his large chestnut eyes glowed as he returned her smile. They stood at the door for a moment quietly taking each other in. Then David walked in and embraced her hard.

'It's good, very good to see you, Lynda.' He held her at arm's length for a moment, looking her up and down. 'You're thinner. Been working too hard?' he queried, and as she nodded drew her to him again. She thought she could smell moist earth, freshly mown grass and she snuggled closer to him, closing her eyes and breathing deeply.

When they separated, he looked concerned.

'Are you all right, Lynda?'

She nodded. 'Just tired.'

Then to stop his inspection of her she offered to show him the flat. Both of them were a little awkward on this unfamiliar territory. She could feel his eyes on her when he thought she wasn't looking. And surreptitiously, she glanced at him, trying to take in this somewhat unfamiliar David.

Lynda racked her mind for things to say. Finally, at a loss, she asked, 'Can I get you a drink? Some tea or coffee?'

David shook his head. 'Strange, isn't it, how uncomfortable we suddenly are with each other.' He put his hand out to her and she took it. 'Driving down here, I was full of the things I wanted to tell you. And now—blank, there's nothing.'

Lynda laughed a little nervously. 'It's just the same for me.'

'I guess we'll have to learn each other all over again.' There was a slight query in his voice as he looked deeply into her eyes. 'If you want to, that is?'

She nodded, then jumped up from the sofa. 'Come on, let's go out and eat. I'm starving! I'll just put some clothes on.'

She was grateful for the momentary respite of her room. She must put Paul out of her mind. That was something she couldn't tell David about. Nor must he notice her preoccupation. She practised a smile in her mirror and, satisfied, went out to join David.

They walked through the wet streets, Lynda pointing out sights of interest on the way.

'Quite the Londoner, aren't you,' he muttered as she led him to a local pizzeria.

'Hardly. I miss the country all the time.'

He looked at her curiously as they sat down at a small round table. 'Come back with me, then. For a few days.'

'I'd love to.' She tasted the idea in her mind. 'I'd *really* love to.' Her eyes clouded. 'But I can't. I've got to finish working on this project.'

With the mention of work, the words began to pour out of her. She told David about the stately homes, about her first drawings and how they'd been criticised, about her meeting with Stanford Rees, and the new drawings which were almost done and were good. She told him about everything except Paul, who was as absent in her words as he was present in her mind.

'But it's all been a terrific strain, and actually, I think I'd like to get out of the whole thing once I've completed this preliminary stage,' she finished.

'It doesn't sound at all like you,' David retorted. 'You're just tired. Why not ask your boss for a week off now?' He took her hand. 'I can take you back with me and show you around all the improvements we've made.'

When Lynda didn't answer, he began to tell her about the work he had been doing on the farm. As he talked, she was gradually overcome by a nostalgia for home.

'I will ask Mr Dunlop,' she suddenly resolved, her eyes sparkling.

David gave her a warm smile. They left the restaurant arm in arm, talking, interrupting each other amicably, laughing as if they'd never been separated. They strolled through the streets for what seemed like miles, sometimes looking about them, sometimes so involved in each other's words that London became invisible. At last Lynda groaned, 'My feet . . .! Let's go home and rest.'

By the time they reached the flat, Tricia was already home from work. She greeted them with surprise and eyed David curiously. Lynda made the necessary introductions, watching Tricia carefully to see how she would respond to David. Somehow, her reaction was important, a kind of hurdle for David to cross.

'Tricia, this is David, my oldest and dearest friend.

David, I've told you about Tricia, my flatmate and guide to London ways.'

The two looked at each other for a moment. Then David gave Tricia a wide slow smile which lit up his broad face.

'Lynda forgot to tell me how beautiful you are.'

Tricia flashed pearly teeth at him engagingly.

'She's been working so hard, she's forgotten to tell me anything. That's why I was so surprised to see you both come in. I thought Lynda was holed up in her room working away. When that door's shut'— she gestured towards Lynda's room—'I can feel DO NOT DISTURB etched there in capital letters.'

'Good thing I've arrived, then, to bring you two together,' David's eyes moved appreciatively from one woman to the other. 'Why don't I take you both out tonight? There's a concert I'd love to go to, and then dinner . . .'

Tricia looked at Lynda to see whether her presence would be an intrusion. Lynda smiled, 'That sounds wonderful, David. As long as I've got time to soak my feet and change.'

He glanced at his watch and nodded. 'Plenty of time. Make yourselves ravishing—I've got to make sure I remember my London nights!'

Tricia poured David a drink, passed him an evening paper and with a murmur of, 'Be patient,' followed Lynda to her room.

'Why have you been hiding *him*?' she whispered as Lynda's door closed behind them. 'I didn't know they still made them as nice as that.'

Lynda smiled gaily, 'I'm glad you approve. David's the older brother I never had. We grew up together.'

Tricia looked at her sceptically, 'Are you sure he's just a brother?'

Lynda shrugged her shoulders.

'Well, I think we should make ourselves 'ravishing' for him. Come and raid my wardrobe. I'm going to *dress* you for a change.'

Tricia's enthusiasm was contagious, and both girls having washed, Lynda allowed herself to be led to Tricia's room.

With the eye of a professional, Tricia took two dresses out of her wardrobe, one a wine-coloured silk with a border of exotic plants flowering out of its hemline; the other a midnight blue sheath with slender shoulder straps made to be worn with a flowing print overblouse, Japanese in flavour.

Lynda's eyes glowed. 'They're beautiful! But I can't wear these. They're ... they're too extravagant.'

Tricia winked. 'Yes, you can. I'm plotting to whisk you and David off to a late party afterwards, show him a little of London life.'

Lynda tried on the dresses, feeling a little like a princess in a fairy-tale as she saw her midnight blue reflection in the mirror. Fairy Godmother Tricia eyed her critically.

'Yes, that one's perfect. Let me do your hair and face as well.' She set to work with obvious enjoyment, and when she'd finished muttered, 'I've obviously missed my calling. Take a look.'

Lynda looked at her transformed self in the long glass. Tricia had outlined her eyes in a luminescent blue, making them into soft mysterious pools, glossed her lips and pulled back her hair on one side with a delicate blue flower grip. 'We can see that wonderful bone structure of yours now,' she had said as she brushed back Lynda's hair. 'Make the best of it.'

'Is that me?' Lynda breathed. 'You *have* missed your calling!'

Tricia smiled as she pulled black satin trousers over her slender hips and topped these with a sheer black and white Indian blouse with wide ruffled sleeves. 'We set each other off well,' she said as she looked at their two forms in the mirror. She brushed her silky blonde hair to a smooth sheen, applied a dab of bright red lipstick and then took out two wraps and passed one to Lynda. 'Ready?'

Lynda nodded and as they emerged from the door said, 'Thanks, Tricia. You're very kind.'

'Don't thank me too soon,' Tricia gave her a meaningful look.

Before Lynda had a chance to grasp what she meant, she heard David gasp.

'Unbelievable!' His eyes shone and he held a large hand to his heart. 'I don't know if I'm strong enough for this—the two most beautiful girls I've ever laid hands on.' His eyes twinkled as he offered them each an arm.

Both girls laughed, and as the three of them went down the stairs, Lynda realised that she had never heard David engaged in this kind of gallantry before. They were obviously parts of him she had never explored. The thought brought a warmth to her face and she gave his arm an involuntary squeeze as he helped her into the taxi.

They were lucky. There were a few tickets still available for the concert David wanted to hear. It was at the Festival Hall, which Lynda had never previously visited, and every time she caught a glimpse of their threesome in one of the long lobby mirrors, she failed to recognise either herself or David. She had always thought of the two of them as gambolling children or dreamy teenagers, but now . . .

She sank farther into the red plush seat and

glanced at David out of the corner of her eye. He was intent on the music, enveloped in the first sweeping strains of the violins, his eyes glowing. She let her thoughts wander as the richness of sound poured over them.

The concert over, they walked out into the clear, bright night air.

'Do you know what I really fancy doing with you two sophisticated ladies?' David drew them into a huddle and paused mysteriously. 'Eating oysters.'

'I know just the place,' Tricia offered. They hailed a taxi and went off to Tricia's favourite oyster bar: waiters in tails speaking in muted tones, chandeliers and green leather. Letting the cool sea and lemon flavour slide down their throats, they bubbled over with laughter.

'I could eat another two dozen,' David muttered playfully, 'but you know what these are supposed to do to my virility . . .' He passed a finger lightly down each of their arms.

Lynda felt a flush rising to her face, but Tricia countered archly, 'Uh-uh, not yet. I'm going to take the two of you off to *my* treat—a party full of bright young things.' She looked at Lynda with mock seriousness. 'We'll have to keep David closely in tow to make sure he's not stolen away from us.'

'Not much chance of that,' he said firmly, and turned to Lynda. 'If you're too tired, I don't mind just taking you home where we can chat quietly.'

Lynda shook her head. 'I'm fine, and you mustn't miss anything.'

They climbed into another taxi and Tricia gave the driver instructions. When they emerged she led them through a narrow lane into an enclosed garden courtyard in the middle of which stood a large brick barn-like structure from which they could hear strongly rhythmical music.

'It's a painter's studio,' she explained. 'The party seems to be well under way.' They walked into a vast single room dimly lit and crowded with people. At the far end of the room Lynda could see musicians, a bass player, guitarist, drummer and pianist, swaying as they played a mellow blues. In front of them couples danced, entwined or separate as their bodies moved to the pulsing sound.

Tricia took them up a circular wrought iron staircase to a plant-filled loft where the girls dropped their wraps. As they walked back down the stairs, Lynda had a clearer picture of people wearing every variety of striking and outlandish clothes, of crimped and Afroed and silky hair, of bare shoulders and silvery textured legs.

'It's what we serious folk call Bohemia,' Tricia said in a loud stage whisper when they were back in the main room. She pointed out some television stars, well-known actors, and then spotted their host.

'Come, I'll introduce you.'

He was a small dark man with bright intelligent eyes who embraced Tricia warmly. Presented to Lynda, he did the same and whispered in her ear, 'Tricia's beautiful friends are always welcome.' He then shook David's hand and took them all off to fetch drinks.

Lynda looked round to see whether she could catch a glimpse of any of his own work. He noticed her intent. 'Never keep any of my own stuff on the walls. I prefer to look at others' work. There are some good things here,' he said casually, and pointed to an oil by a painter she had always admired.

She went to look at it more closely, leaving the others behind her. Suddenly she felt an arm around her shoulder, a hand stroking the thin material of her blouse. Her pulse quickened and her mouth grew dry. Without looking up she knew immediately who it was: Paul. She veered round to escape from his arm and confronted his steely blue eyes. There was a derisive twist to his lips.

'A little jumpy tonight, and rude as always, Miss Harrow.'

Her eyes blazed, but no words came to her and she turned to walk away. He put an arm out to stop her and caught her by the shoulder. 'Not so fast, Lynda,' his voice was huskily grim. 'You can't always be running out on me.' He manoeuvred her firmly towards the band and then turned her to face him. 'We should at least dance with each other once before you decide to walk out on me.'

He drew her to him, crushing her breasts against the soft velvet of his jacket and burying his face in her hair. She could smell the whisky on his breath mixed with the rough odour of Gitanes. 'He's drunk,' she thought, but despite herself her body moulded itself to his. She could feel his hand taut on the base of her spine pressing her to him, shaping her to his firmness. She closed her eyes and allowed herself to sway against him. He relaxed his hold a little, giving her room to move more freely to the pulsing rhythm that enveloped them both. Then she felt his hands cupping her face. She opened her eyes to meet his gazing at her.

'Not so bad, is it?' he whispered, drawing her close again. She melted against him only to be wakened by a drawling female voice.

'Paul, there you are! I've been looking all over for you. It was wonderful tonight. The audience loved us!'

Lynda turned to draw away, wishing she could vanish rather than meet the owner of the voice. But

Paul kept one arm firmly around her.

'Lynda, have you met Vanessa—Vanessa Tarn?'

Lynda muttered a greeting, taking in Vanessa's lavishness; and then stumbling out, 'I've got to get back to my friends,' she moved away, only to hear Vanessa stage whisper, 'Not quite your type, is she, darling? A little plain,' as she moved into the circle of Paul's arms.

Lynda walked blindly in the direction she vaguely remembered having left David and Tricia. She wanted nothing more than to leave immediately, to leave it all—Paul, work, London.

'Lynda, Lynda!' she heard a voice at her side and turned to face David. 'You looked right through us and walked past.' He eyed her curiously.

'Sorry, I was daydreaming,' she forced a smile. 'I guess I'm tired.'

'Would you like to go?'

Lynda looked at him a little blankly, then shook her head. She wasn't ready to face David on his own just yet.

He guided her back towards Tricia, who was talking to the painter and to Robert.

'Hello, gorgeous.' Robert planted a firm kiss on either side of her cheeks. 'Enjoying yourself?' Lynda nodded. 'I like your friend,' he smiled warmly at David and winked at her.

'And I like yours,' David parried, giving Tricia an exaggerated ogle. They all laughed warmly and Lynda tried to lose herself in their cheerful banter. But Tricia motioned her aside and they walked a few steps away from the men towards a large abstract canvas covered with black and red patches.

'I just wanted your opinion on this,' Tricia said in a loud voice by way of explanation. Then more softly, 'What's up between you and Paul Overton? I saw the two of you dancing and I thought if you got any closer you'd melt into each other.' She looked at Lynda ruefully. 'Are you falling for him?'

Lynda shook her head vigorously, but she could feel her cheeks burning. Tricia's look was sceptical.

'Well, be careful. He's been around, you know, and I imagine he's hard to resist. Incidentally, I kept David occupied so he wouldn't notice. I thought he might be hurt.'

Lynda mumbled vague thanks. 'God, I'm so tired I'd like to be in bed right now. Perhaps David could stay on with you. I don't want to drag him away.'

But David would have none of it. He too was quite ready to leave. Tricia called a taxi for them and they set off into the cool night air, Lynda keeping her eyes well lowered all the while, terrified that she might yet again have to confront Paul. David was silent until they were snugly seated in the back of the taxi, then, in a voice which brought back all her childhood in a flash, he asked softly,

'What is it, Lynda, what's wrong?'

She could feel the tears pouring out of her, the sobs building up uncontrollably. He put his arm round her shoulders and drew her close, holding her there until the tears died down.

Finally she found a quavering voice. 'I don't know, David, but I think—I think I'd like to go home with you. If only I can.'

CHAPTER SIX

THE lush green of fertile Shropshire hills stretched
out below them as David's car slowly climbed a steep
incline. Lynda opened her window wide and let the
soft rain moisten her face. She breathed deeply,
giving out a slow luxurious sigh. The rough-hewn
grey stone houses, the brown and white dots of cows,
gave her an enormous sense of wellbeing.

'Oh, David, I'm so happy to be here! It feels as if
I've been away for ever.'

She could see the smile on his face, but he said
nothing as he concentrated on the twists and bends
in the narrow road.

Lynda relaxed deeply into the car seat and gazed
out along the side of the road. Each break in the
trees, each bend, provided a new perspective. She
could feel the tensions of the last few months gradually leaving her body and she felt like leaping up
and running out on one of those smooth green fields.

It had been very kind of Mr Dunlop to let her
take the time off. Days seemed to have passed since
she had confronted him with her demand for a holiday, but it was only a little over twenty-four hours.
She had finished all the drawings to do with the first
two houses and walked into his office early on the
Tuesday morning, hoping beyond hope that Paul
would not yet be in.

'Oh, good, Lynda,' he'd said, 'I've been looking
forward to seeing these. Paul told me on Friday how
well the work was going and how pleased he was
with you.' He had given her just a hint of a wink.

'He even managed to say that I'd been right about you.'

Lynda had felt herself flushing and before she could lose her nerve, had blurted out, 'Mr Dunlop, I'm exhausted. Do you think I could have a little time off now to go home for a bit of a rest?'

Mr Dunlop had eyed her kindly. 'You do look a little peaked. Yes, yes, why not ... though it's slightly irregular. Still, if Paul is pleased with you, then yes. Take the rest of the week, a little more if you feel you need it.'

She had murmured her thanks and gone away somewhat ungraciously, still afraid if she spent too much time in the office she would bump into Paul. And as she emerged from Mr Dunlop's room, sure enough, there he was. Luckily, he had been deep in conversation with one of the other architects and had only nodded absentmindedly in her direction. She had hurried out of the office, without even saying a word to Tricia, extravagantly taken a taxi to the flat, packed a few things and left a note. Then David had come to pick her up and they were off, slowly, almost like tourists, planning an attractive route, stopping overnight in a small inn.

Now, as she sat looking out of the car window, Lynda felt a little ashamed of her own cowardice. She had not breathed a word to Mr Dunlop about perhaps not continuing with the stately homes project. And running away from Paul like that was silly. Still—she shuddered a little—she couldn't have faced him in cool daylight with the memory of her most recent humiliation, the imprint of his body still etched on hers. No wonder he thought her brazen if each time he touched her, she simply succumbed!

'Dreaming again?' David's voice intruded on her thoughts. 'We're almost there.'

She looked at him in profile, the strong jaw, the shock of unruly sandy hair, his large hands on the steering wheel, and felt strangely safe. He turned in response to her gaze and seeing her look, reached for her hand and grasped it firmly.

The rain had cleared and the setting sun enveloped everything about them in a rosy haze. At the bottom of the winding road, Lynda could make out the cluster of small buildings which made up the farm. How lovely it all looked, like something out of a children's storybook. Her heart beat faster.

As they drove slowly closer, she could see the two brown horses peacefully grazing in the field above the house, the tall oaks sheltering the garden in which they had played hide and seek, the murky green of the tiny pond where she had always expected the frogs to turn into princes.

David pulled the car up behind the barn and they stepped out. Lynda took a deep breath, revelling in the rich aroma of hay and cows and moist earth. It felt like a recurring dream, intensely familiar yet strangely unreal. So much had happened since she had last been here, yet there were her mother's bright yellow roses climbing busily all over the front of the house, the worn, colourful curtains framing the small kitchen window, the slightly crooked front door made of deeply grained oak. She wanted to pinch herself to make sure she was really here.

A man she didn't recognise suddenly appeared as if from nowhere, and David greeted him warmly and made introductions. It was the new hand he had hired, who now lived in the tiny cottage at the far end of the cluster of buildings. While he and David exchanged information about work, Lynda let herself into the house.

The kitchen was unchanged, except perhaps for

something less of a clutter on tables and shelves, but the old, slightly chipped blue and white vase was there, full of bright garden dahlias. Mrs Wood, who came in to help with the housework, must have seen to that. Nothing had been altered in the beamed drawing-room either, except that there was a new stereo and a mass of records, neatly stacked. Of course, David was now living in the house. Lynda had known it, though she hadn't quite taken it in as a reality. The thought disturbed her slightly, but she put it away as she climbed up the narrow staircase towards her room

. There it was, tucked under an eave, the small bed neatly covered with the comforter she herself had made a cover for at the age of fourteen—tiny mauve and white flowers that had made her feel she was sleeping in the garden. Her bedraggled Teddy was perched on top of it, looking at her with eyes slightly askew. She gave him a friendly poke and sat down on the bed. On the walls hung the drawings and watercolours she had done throughout the years: random, unframed, attached with drawing pins, simply her favourites at various points in time. Between the table and small bookcase were more, stacked in folders.

She lay down, letting her eyes wander round the room, taking in details. At least Paul's presence couldn't follow her here. But as soon as she framed the thought, an aching sensation flooded her limbs, a pit seemed to yawn at the base of her stomach. She trembled; the sense of Paul standing over her was so acute that he invaded the room, making its atmosphere impossible to breathe.

Lynda got off the bed and walked briskly down-stairs. She could hear David moving round in the kitchen and the strains of Sibelius filling the house.

She felt like turning it off, but didn't dare.

David was looking into the oven when she walked in.

'Mrs Wood has left us some stew. I rang her to say we'd be coming tonight.' He looked at her questioningly, 'Are you all right? Would you like a drink?'

Lynda nodded. 'It feels odd having you offer me a drink rather than the other way round.' She had said it without thinking and she could see hurt registering in his kind face.

'I'm sorry, I hadn't thought.' He looked deeply into her eyes. 'You know, I live here now, most of the time anyway, except when I go home to help Father out and keep him company. It makes the work easier . . . I thought you'd realised.'

She smiled, 'I did know, David. I just hadn't quite taken it in. And I'm glad. It would be awful to think of the house empty.'

He handed her a glass of sherry, grazing her hand as he did so. They both seemed to have the same thought simultaneously.

'I could go back to Father's tonight,' he said. 'I had thought of it.'

She looked at him for a moment, then shook her head vigorously, touching the locket round her neck. 'No, I'd be terrified of being here all alone.'

The last time Lynda had been home after her mother's death, both her sisters had been in the house. Together they had sorted out her mother's belongings, given her clothes away, arranged her room so she wasn't altogether absent nor too depressingly present. But now Caroline was back with her husband and two children in York, and Sarah, the middle sister, was working as a solicitor's secretary in the county town some forty miles away. They would see each other at the weekend, she hoped.

'Which room are you using?' Lynda asked.

'Come, I'll show you.' David drained his sherry and she followed him upstairs. He had taken over the guestroom and had made it very much his own, replacing the flowery curtains with a brown blind and painting the walls a matt white. His books and magazines were scattered everywhere and she recognised the old armchair he had brought from home. She went to sit in it.

'It feels good, all this,' she commented, 'like the old days.'

He beamed a smile at her. 'I'm glad you approve. I must say I was just a little worried.' He sat on the bed quietly for a few moments, then said, 'I'm off to pay the cows a visit. Would you like to come?'

'Oh yes.'

They went downstairs and Lynda pulled on a pair of old wellingtons which still stood in a box by the side door, as if waiting for her return. The thick woolly sweater her mother had knitted ages ago was there too, hanging on a hook, and she put it on. Then she laughed gaily at David, 'I'm ready.'

Looking at her, he laughed back, 'Quite a change from London!' And as they walked out of the door, he put his arm tenderly round her shoulder.

The next few days passed in a haze of near-perfect wellbeing. Lynda rode her mare, sometimes alone, sometimes with David, over all the familiar haunts, reappropriating each lane, each tree. She visited David's father, happy to see him again. She let her hair go wild and wavy in the moist windy air and she never seemed to emerge from her jeans and old sweater.

While David worked, she walked off alone and explored, taking her watercolours and pad with her and sketching for hours on end. She helped him with the cows, wondering whether her fingers would remember how to milk them gently and feeling thrilled when they did. Her cheeks grew pink from the exercise, her eyes brighter than they had been for months. In the evenings, she and David sat on the rug in front of the blazing fire, eating their food there, listening to music and talking, until they were both almost asleep. Then David would kiss her gently on the forehead and wish her goodnight.

But beneath it all there was a sense of expectation, almost of trepidation. Lynda felt that David wanted to speak to her about her plans, about them, but whenever he led up to anything of the kind, she turned the conversation elsewhere, forestalled him. He was patient, but she knew the moment would have to come and she had no idea what she would say. At night, when she lay down in her girlhood bed and closed her eyes, she would immediately feel Paul's arms around her, his charged presence almost suffocating her. And her dreams were full of him, agonising dreams in which he held her tightly, breathlessly, only to vanish suddenly into the arms of another woman.

One day, too, she had decided to walk to the local village to greet old acquaintances and pick up some extra food. Invariably, they had all treated her kindly, but invariably too, they had all treated her as if she were something of a foreigner, suspicious that she might judge them; ready, too, to judge her and condemn or congratulate her on her successes and failures. When Mrs Peabody had said to her, 'Home to stay, then?' she had baulked, 'No, just a visit.'

'Managing well in London, are you?' Mrs Peabody had asked mistrustfully.

'Oh yes, rather,' Lynda had said definitively, expressing an assurance she didn't altogether feel in an accent not altogether her own. She remembered then how her mother had always kept her distance from the villagers, unwilling to let her family become material for their tongues.

On Saturday David had said to her, 'Let's have a meal out this evening. They've opened a French restaurant in one of the pubs not too far away. It will make a change.'

Lynda had nodded agreement and in anticipation of a night out she had washed her hair, ironed a dress and polished her shoes.

'I'd forgotten you had legs,' David smiled as she came into the drawing room. She lifted her skirt demurely above her knees and twirled round. 'Two,' she bantered back.

He came towards her and enveloped her in his strong arms. She raised her face to his and for the first time since her arrival he kissed her long and hard. She let him, and found her arms moving up to embrace him, her lips returning his kiss. They stood like that for a long time, then letting her go, David said lightly, only his eyes betraying the intensity of his emotion, 'I should have done that before.'

Lynda lowered her eyes, wanting to hide from him a little. She had enjoyed his kiss, its warmth. Yet behind it there had been the memory of Paul. It had frightened her. Would she ever be able to erase it from her mind?

David was looking at her quizzically now, as if he wanted to say something more. But instead he simply took her arm and with a mock threat in his voice said, 'To be continued after dinner.'

They went out to the car and drove silently for a while. Then in a strangely muted voice David said,

'Lynda, there's something I've been wanting to talk to you about for a while now, but I don't know quite how to begin.'

She braced herself for it, wishing all the while that he wouldn't speak, that he would wait. But she said nothing.

'It's difficult,' he continued, waiting for her to make a sign.

But she only made herself small in the corner of the seat and waited. They drove along a little farther and finally he said, 'It's about your mother and father.'

Lynda gasped, thoroughly astonished, all attention now.

'What is it, David?'

He chuckled wryly, 'Not what you were expecting, is it?'

She could feel herself flushing in the dark, 'I'm sorry David, I . . .'

'It's all right,' he took her hand and squeezed it hard, 'we'll get to that too. But this first, and I really *don't* know where to begin. I've been thinking it over for months.'

'Please, David, begin anywhere!'

He pulled off the main road into a small drive which led to the pub. 'Let's have a drink first and order dinner. It will loosen my tongue.'

Lynda was filled with a dire premonition. She let him lead her to a table, drank down a gin and tonic quickly and paid no attention to the menu. When the first course arrived, she couldn't bear any more small talk.

'Please, David, tell me!' she begged.

He looked at her steadily and poured each of them a glass of red wine. Then he took a large gulp.

'Right—no tears, no hysterics. That's one of the reasons I wanted to tell you outside the house.'

Lynda gripped the arms of her chair and listened tensely.

'Just before your mother died—you remember the two of us were very close in those days, since all of you were away—she called me in one evening after work, made me sit down with a drink and announced that she had something important to tell me. It was to be a secret between us until at least a year after her death. She knew by then that she would go quite soon. I don't know why she stipulated at least a year—perhaps she thought you would judge her less harshly with time. In any case, I vowed secrecy. It's now well over a year, but I wanted to get you in the right frame of mind, in the right place.'

He took a bite of food and drank a little more wine. 'And I've been a little cowardly. What she told me was that your father hadn't been dead all those years. Only as good as, as far as she was concerned.'

Lynda gasped outright. 'But where is he?'

'He's dead now,' David said quietly. 'I think that's why she talked to me. She'd just had news of his death from America.' He paused, watching Lynda's face, her air of utter disbelief.

'I know you're thinking how could she have, she who was so honest, so upright. Well, it must have been very hard for her and I think she probably never stopped tormenting herself with it. You were probably about one year old when it all happened.'

He paused. 'This is all going to sound terribly blunt, but we can fill in what details I know later. Your mother was pregnant. She knew, somehow, that it was for the last time, and she desperately wanted a male child. Your father already felt burdened with the three of you—there wasn't much money about—so there was friction between them. One night he came home in a terrible temper—he'd had too much to drink, something had gone wrong with banking arrangements. In any case, they had a row, and he hit her. She tripped over a rug and fell down the stairs. Miraculously, she didn't break anything, but she did miscarry.'

David stopped to examine Lynda's face.

'Go on,' she urged, 'go on.'

'Well, that's the crux of it, really. When she was better she told him to leave. She wanted nothing more to do with him. He went.'

'Just like that?' Lynda voiced her disbelief.

'Your mother didn't go into intimate details . . . My sense was that he probably tried to make it up, but she was too proud, too stiffnecked. And then, after that, he went. Or so it would seem, for she heard nothing from him in over a year. After a couple of months of total silence, she announced his death. She'd already let it be known that he was away in the United States, doing something or other. Then all she had to say was that he'd been involved in a car crash.'

Lynda moved her food round her plate, unable to swallow a mouthful. Her mind, her emotions were in a jumble. She wanted to ask her mother a hundred questions, to console her for the pain she must have suffered; but also to rage—yes, to scream at her for being too proud, for having deprived them of a father. She couldn't bring her eyes to meet David's for a moment. Then she mumbled, 'She must have regretted her decision terribly.'

David shrugged, 'I don't know. I think she did at the last. That's why she didn't feel strong enough to tell you all herself. But that's not the end. After a year, she had a letter from him, in America. She'd guessed correctly. He asked after the children, but nothing directly of her, and he sent a cheque. She didn't answer, didn't cash the cheque, though the money would have been very useful.

'The following year another letter came, much the same as the first, but bearing a larger cheque. Still she made no sign. And the next year again, establishing a pattern that was to continue. The letters, she soon noticed, were always written at the same time, the date of their wedding anniversary. She never took the money, never replied—God knows why. Perhaps by that time she was paralysed by guilt.

'Then for some reason, she didn't say why, about a year before her death she wrote to him, a long letter, she told me, telling him about the three of you, about herself, and the farm, about what she'd said of him and how she had never tarnished his image before you—asking in a way, I think, for forgiveness. This time there was no reply from him, but about two months later a thick envelope arrived bearing the stamp of a legal firm. She told me she knew instantly what it contained, and she was right. It was news of his death. He had died in a car crash and his will left everything to the three of you.'

David stopped to take a deep breath. 'I think it was the fatality of it all, the way she felt she had somehow determined the mode of his death all those years ago, that hastened her own.'

Tears were streaming down Lynda's face. She thought of her father, the dashing young man in the Air Force uniform she knew from a few fuzzy wartime photographs. She couldn't reconcile that face with any of this. And her mother—the horror of it, the strength of her secrecy, of her will.

David took a handkerchief from his pocket and wiped her tears. 'Try to think of it as a strange love story,' he said gently. 'After all, in however distant a way they were linked only to each other over all those years.'

Lynda tried a watery smile. The waitress, on David's instruction, had brought some strong black coffee and Lynda now gulped it down. She was full of questions she couldn't yet put words to, so she asked, 'Do Sarah and Caroline know about this yet?'

David nodded, 'I told them before I came up to London. They wanted me to tell you and it was one of the main reasons for my coming. But then I couldn't bring myself to say anything there. You felt so nervy and . . . well, amidst all those strangers, I felt a stranger too.' He took her hand. 'It's hard to imagine, your mother and all those years of tenacious secrecy.'

'I guess that's why she kept saying men weren't to be trusted. I could never work it out. I had no idea where the edge of bitterness came from.'

'Well, now we know. I guess at the beginning she thought he might still come back any day. And when he didn't she steeled her will against him.'

'Yes,' Lynda reflected, 'they must both have been stubbornly strong-willed . . . I don't know what's happened to mine.'

Unreasonably, thoughts of London had suddenly flooded back, and she felt drained. She couldn't go on . . . go on working with Paul day in, day out.

David looked at her oddly. 'What are you talking about, Lynda? You've got a will of iron! Look at the way you insisted on art school, then packed yourself off to London leaving us all behind . . . And now— well, I simply don't understand you sometimes.'

She lowered her eyes. How can you understand?

she thought to herself. I'm developing a secrecy almost as astute as mother's. Out loud, she said, 'That was before. Now . . . now I just want to give it all up, do nothing for a while.' Her lips trembled and she could feel the tears rushing to her eyes again.

'I'll take you home,' David said, 'and you can have a good cry. It's a lot to take in all at once. And we can talk about London,' he added threateningly.

Lynda went out to the car while he paid the bill. She didn't even try now to stop the flow of tears, and she lost herself in them so totally that, without being aware of how it had happened, she next found herself snuggled into the sofa in front of the fire at home with David's arm wrapped tightly around her. He lifted her face to his and kissed her tears away gently, and then more forcefully found her mouth. She clung to him, to his kiss, his warmth, the strength she could feel surging through him. After some moments, he pulled himself away with a visible effort, and took her hands in his.

'I don't want to take unfair advantage of you now,' he smiled, but there was a look of sadness in his eyes.

'Oh David,' she moved herself into the circle of his arms again, 'what should I do? Tell me. And I will.'

He held her close. 'I know what I'd like.'

'What?' She felt she knew what he would say, and she was ready to let him set the pace.

'I'd like you to stay, now, here, with me, for good.' He paused. 'But I don't feel that's altogether right.'

Lynda was surprised and she tried to withdraw from his arms, but he held her tight.

'I somehow, oh I don't know, I don't feel you're ready. When I saw you in London, when you talked about your work, I realised how important it all was for you, that you had to see at least the project you're working on through, no matter how you feel now.'

She smiled at him as she had done in the old days, 'Wise David,' she said.

'And then there's something else. I don't quite know what it is . . . A distance. Another man, perhaps.' He looked at her steadily and she blanched. 'Am I right then?'

Lynda shook her head vehemently. 'No, there's no one, at least nothing real,' she stammered it out and wrenching herself away began to pace in front of the fireplace.

David watched her for a moment and then said softly, 'I'll wait you know, for a little while, at least.'

She turned towards him and coming close placed a soft kiss on his smooth lips. Then she mouthed a goodnight and climbed slowly up the stairs.

As she snuggled under her sheets, Lynda thought how good, how kind, how reasonable David was in comparison to Paul with his tempestuous moods. She shuddered. But there was no help for it now. She had near enough been ordered back into the fray. And David was right: she would have to steel herself to it, be strong, like her mother. And her last waking thoughts were about this extraordinary woman whom she now felt she had never known adequately.

Sunday morning dawned bright and clear and Lynda woke to the smell of sizzling bacon. She got out of bed, feeling ravenous, and only when she had pulled some clothes on and was going down the stairs did she begin to remember what had occurred on the previous evening. But now her parents' story filled her with something akin to awe. She went into the kitchen where David stood over the cooker.

'Imagine her, day in, day out working in this house and stubbornly guarding her secret. It's amazing!'

He turned to her and smiled, his eyes warm. 'I can see you've had a good night's sleep. I was going to bring breakfast up to you, thinking you'd be shattered . . .'

She looked at him closely. His features were drawn, his face pale beneath the ruddy colouring.

'Oh, David, I'm sorry! You're the one who's exhausted. You've been carrying the burden for us all. I've been so selfish.' Lynda put her arms around him and buried her head in his shoulder. He stroked her hair and whispered humorously, 'Like an old married couple already, the two of us.'

They both laughed and sat down to eat, happy in each other's presence. Lynda felt that somehow after last night the air between them had been cleared. She was full of energy.

'Let's set off for Sarah's early. I'm dying to hear what she has to say about Mother and Father.'

After an enormous breakfast of bacon and eggs and thick slices of toast and pots of coffee, they set off across the sunny countryside. Lynda stored up images, thinking to herself that she might not be back here for some time. David drove slowly, steadily, singing old songs all the while and soon Lynda joined him. By the time they arrived, they were both beaming at each other.

Lynda had never before visited the cottage Sarah now lived in and she was curious about her sister's new life. The two had been close until Lynda went off to art school, but they were quintessentially different. Sarah was small, with thick curly blonde hair and a wonderfully rounded figure. She was totally reliable, efficient and quick-witted, and although there was only a little over a year between them, she treated Lynda like a vagrant younger sister whose dreaminess needed occasional stern mothering. Lynda allowed it, knowing that Sarah meant well, but knowing too that she was quite capable of drawing the line and telling Sarah not to interfere.

Sarah opened the door before they had had a chance to ring the bell and the two sisters hugged each other warmly and then stepped back to examine one another.

'You haven't changed at all,' Sarah said. 'Well, perhaps a little thinner, and you're still not dressing properly. I thought you'd appear in some extraordinary London get-up.'

Lynda smiled down at her worn jeans, 'I left all that in London. But you look wonderful.' And Sarah did, in a pretty print dress that accentuated her slender waist and curves.

'You do indeed,' she heard David echoing behind her as he moved to greet Sarah in turn. She blushed a bright crimson and Lynda chuckled to herself. Sarah had always blushed when David paid her a compliment.

She ushered them in, showing Lynda the four tiny rooms all painted in tasteful pastels and full of the bric-à-brac Sarah loved. They sat down in the lemon and white drawing-room while Sarah went out to make some tea. She returned carrying a delicate china teapot and dainty cups on a large tray. Handing Lynda a cup, she looked at her enquiringly.

'What do you make of David's story about Mother?'

'Astounding,' Lynda replied. 'And now that I've slept on it, I think that Mother was truly remarkable . . . though I do regret not having known Father.'

'And I do. It makes one a little too independent, not ever having had a man around.' She turned her clear grey eyes a little wistfully on David. Lynda caught the glance and a suspicion began to form in her mind, but she put it aside. Instead she replied truthfully.

'I don't know. That's been important to me. Every time I feel life is getting on top of me, I think of Mother and how she managed and I carry on. Well, almost every time . . .' It was her turn to look at David.

He grinned, 'Tell Sarah about the project you're working on.'

Lynda did, embroidering it with anecdotes about her trip to the Shaw home. She was careful never to mention Paul, whose name and presence she had to chase away at every turn. It made her a little breathless.

But of course Sarah asked, 'Any exciting men?' She looked first at Lynda and then briefly at David.

Lynda was ready. 'Oh, lots. I have to chase them away with sticks.' She refused to meet David's eye and coloured.

He stood up. 'Well, if you two are going to start in on that, I'll go and have a look at the garden.'

'Oh no,' they both said together, entreating him to stay, and Sarah quickly turned the conversation to other things, her own job, the friends she had made in town. Then she suggested that Lynda and David have a walk while she got lunch together. 'A real Sunday dinner,' she emphasised. 'And I don't like anyone helping.'

'Sarah seems to be thriving,' Lynda observed as she and David strolled idly round the empty marketplace and up to the old castle walls.

David murmured agreement.

'She's very fond of you, isn't she?' The thought had suddenly occurred to Lynda in a new light.

He looked at her strangely. 'If you mean what I think you mean, I don't know. I hadn't thought about it. I'm very fond of *her*,' he added as an afterthought.

Lynda was smitten by a sudden pang of jealousy. She had never conceived of David with any woman but herself. So selfish, she chided herself. And now, as she glanced at him with another's eyes, she could see that his rugged solidity was very attractive. She caught hold of his arm and squeezed it, then guiltily drew away. Did it really take the presence of another woman to make her appreciate David?

Lynda secretly watched Sarah and him throughout the long Sunday dinner and she concluded that Sarah was nurturing a secret passion. She had prepared a splendid dinner, like those enormous meals their mother had made on a Sunday: roast, crunchy golden potatoes, heaps of vegetables, gooseberry tart and custard. She served David with special care, making sure he wanted nothing, attentive to his smallest movement, but covertly observing any gesture he made towards Lynda.

At one point, Lynda caught her in the act, and when the sisters' eyes met, Sarah flushed and turned abruptly away. It made Lynda quite certain that she was right, and despite herself, she began to flirt openly with David. She was sorry she hadn't dressed better. The thought that she couldn't count on him left her with a dawning sense of loss.

When it was time to go, she found herself eyeing him suspiciously as he kissed Sarah warmly goodbye. Yes, she was sure of it; if she absented herself long enough, the two of them would make a match of it.

Lynda was pleased to have him all to herself in the car.

'It's going to be hard to go back to London after all this,' she said, almost hoping that David would dissuade her.

'It doesn't have to be for long . . .'

She was only a little reassured by his tone.

'Do you know what I'd like this evening?' she turned to face his profile. 'I'd like you to play for me. You haven't, you know, not since I've been here.'

He gave her a bright smile, 'I thought you'd be bored . . . I'd love to.' He reached for her hand and gave it a quick squeeze and she moved closer to him.

When they walked into the house, Lynda saw a brown envelope on the floor—a telegram. She picked it up and noticing it was for her tore it open with trepidation, while David looked over her shoulder.

'Orders from on top. Come back immediately. Tricia.'

Lynda read the message nervously. She had hoped to go back on Tuesday, but now she would have to rush back to London tomorrow.

'I wonder what that's all about?' she mused.

'I guess they can't get on without you.' David smiled at her comfortingly. 'But you can't do anything until tomorrow, so there's no point fretting. Meanwhile, let's enjoy our last evening.'

He went into the kitchen and came back with a bottle of wine which he uncorked.

'Here, drink some of this. I've been saving it. I'll just see to the animals first.'

Lynda took a sip and then busied herself with

making up a fire. She was certain the telegram had to do with Paul. She could sense his imperiousness in Tricia's 'Orders from on top'. The thought of it made her bristle and she closed herself against him. The nerve of it! She gave the fire a jab with the poker, making the logs tumble and leap with flame.

'Angry about something?' David stood behind her. She jumped up, surprised, her face flushed from the fire.

'The orders from on top,' she said, making a face.

'Suits you, being angry.' He took her hand, led her to the sofa and handed her her glass. Then he looked at her for a long moment and shrugged.

'You're already in London.'

'Oh, David, I'm sorry, it's just that . . .'

He cut her off. 'It doesn't matter.' But he looked annoyed.

'Will you play for me?' Lynda asked.

He sat down at the piano and struck some angry chords. Then he played through a Beethoven sonata in an accelerated tempo, ending up with a thundering crescendo. When he lifted his hands from the piano, they both laughed.

'That should set the cows stampeding,' Lynda commented wryly.

His chestnut eyes crinkled at the corners as he smiled. 'Just sit here for a minute. I've got something for you,' he said, bounding up the stairs and coming back almost immediately. 'I was saving this for our last night together, and this is it, I guess. I've wanted to give you this for some time.' He placed a delicate golden ring with an old-fashioned diamond setting on her third finger. 'It was my mother's.'

Lynda gasped, 'It's beautiful, David, but . . . but I can't really take it.'

He looked into her eyes. 'I want you to have it. It

doesn't tie you to anything. It's—well, it's an ac-knowledgment of all we've shared. And perhaps a promise . . .'

'It belongs here, then,' she said, taking the ring from her finger and threading it on to the chain which bore her mother's locket, 'next to my heart.'

She raised her lips to his and they met in a long warm kiss.

CHAPTER SEVEN

LYNDA heard the familiar 'beep, beep, beep', pushed her coin into the slot and asked for Tricia. Her train had been delayed by an hour and it seemed pointless to go into the office so late in the day. Then, too, she felt drained by the journey, depressed by the grey tawdriness of the station, the swarm of unseeing faces around her.

It seemed a very long time ago that London's bustle had provided her with a thrill, heightened by a tingling fear of its unknown vastness. Now she only wanted to disappear into the repose of her flat and muster her forces for an imminent battle with Paul. At least that was what her long hours of musing on the train had led her to expect.

'Hello, Lynda, where are you?' Tricia's voice crackled over the telephone.

'I'm back—at the station, at least. What's up?'

'It's Paul Overton,' Tricia spoke the name quietly. 'He's gunning for you. You'd better get over here right away.'

'It's too late now. Tell him I'll ring him from the flat.' Lynda was relieved that the return of the 'beep, beep, beeps' prevented Tricia from arguing further and she hung up.

She took a taxi home, ran a bath as soon as she was in the door and then, feeling she could no longer put it off, rang Paul. He was out of the office. She relaxed into her bath with a sigh of relief and then, as she rinsed the foaming shampoo out of her hair, lectured herself sternly. There was no earthly reason for her to be afraid of confronting him. After all, she had had permission from Mr Dunlop for her holiday.

She wrapped her hair in a large towel and rubbed herself dry. 'I must stop behaving like a frightened mouse,' she admonished her mirror image.

The doorbell rang shattering her reverie. She automatically pulled on her towelling robe, but then stopped in her tracks. Why bother answering? Whoever it was would come back if it were important. And Tricia must have her key. But the doorbell pealed insistently again and again. She marched to answer it, shouting, 'All right, I'm coming!'

She swung open the door ready to reprimand whoever was there, then her face fell. There stood Paul, looking for all the world as if he were ready to throttle her. He glowered as he strode past her into the room and with no word of greeting, flung the folio he was carrying on to the sofa. Then he turned on her.

'Where the hell did you run off to without warning?' He glared at her, his eyes blazing as he passed a long-fingered hand through his thick dark hair.

Lynda pulled the gown more tightly round her. She didn't dare meet the charge of his eyes and concentrated instead on the top button of his creamy shirt and the taut muscles of his throat just above it. She shivered. Her voice seemed to come from a long way off.

'I did speak to Mr Dunlop.'

'Mr Dunlop . . .' he breathed sardonically. Then he boomed out, 'You're working with me, not with Mr Dunlop! I—Tricia and I—have been trying to trace you for days!'

Lynda remembered that she hadn't specified to Tricia where she was going. It hadn't seemed necessary, but now she flushed. 'I'm sorry,' she murmured, 'I didn't realise . . .' She raised her eyes to his face, noticing the tension in his jaw, the long angry line of his smooth lips.

He seemed to look at her for the first time, taking in her towel-wrapped hair, and as his eyes travelled downward, the powder blue robe she held clenched tightly round her, her bare legs. He turned away and began to pace round the room.

'Go and get dressed, will you?' she heard him mutter. 'I'm only human!'

Lynda stood fixed to her spot, unable to make her limbs obey her will. Then she felt him looming behind her, felt a single finger moving gently along the exposed nape of her neck, lips delicately brushing the area the finger had touched. She shivered, aware that her every nerve was quivering, that the entire expanse of her body responded to his touch. With an enormous effort she impelled herself towards her room, closing the door softly behind her.

She sat down on her bed for a moment to still her pulse, gain control of her senses. Now she knew why she had been afraid to confront Paul. During her week away she had so pushed the memory of him into the background that she had forgotten the impact of his presence, the sheer animal force of him. She could cope with his anger, his bullying about work, but not with the lithe precision of his movements, the oddly dark vitality of his deep-set blue eyes.

Perhaps if I stay in here long enough, he'll just go away, she thought to herself. But she knew better. She forced herself to take a dress out of her wardrobe, a pair of black tights from her drawer. As she pulled the clothes on, she felt her body tingling, strangely alive. Maybe I should just give in, the thought leapt

violently to the forefront of her mind. But before she
could face it squarely the image of a radiant Vanessa
possessively taking hold of Paul and murmuring,
'Not quite your type . . .' bounded in on her. Her
stomach heaved dizzily. She wouldn't give in to him
just to be used, for a few encounters. No. She touched
the locket round her neck and her fingers met a new
object—the ring. She flushed painfully. Her mother
and David would give her strength, keep her in
hand. She would not be played with lightly. If only
she could still her body!

She tried to brush some order into her wet hair.
Each brush stroke, she felt, added a new link in her
armour against Paul. Finally she considered herself
ready, and composing her face, she walked out to
him.

He was sitting back in the sofa, gazing reflectively
at the glass of whisky he held in his hand. He seemed
lost in thought, oblivious to her presence. Lynda sat
down at the other end of the sofa and his eyes met
hers briefly. Ruefully he looked away.

'I helped myself to a drink. I hope you don't
mind.' His tone was polite, distant.

She shook her head.

'Shall I fix you one?'

'I'll get it.' She was happy to be able to get up
again.

As she put some ice into a glass, he asked, 'Where
did you go?'

'Home. I felt I needed a rest.' She turned back
towards him and sat down.

'Where's home?' She told him. 'Why didn't you
tell me you were going?'

Lynda shrugged. 'It was a last-minute decision
and you weren't around.' She lied a little and then
asked defiantly, 'What's all this fuss about getting

me back here for? I've finished the work.'

'That's what you think, young lady.' He said it humorously, but with a veiled threat in his voice. 'First of all there are these drawings to touch up,' he pointed to two drawings he had drawn out of the folio. They were the last two she had done. 'Then there are the others to get started on.' He paused. 'You aren't going to walk out on this now, are you?' There was a hint of entreaty in his voice as he met her eyes.

Lynda looked down at her drink and shook her head. 'No, I'll see the project through. Well, I'll try anyway,' she said quietly.

'Good, good.' His face lit up and he smiled. Lynda was astonished at the sudden pleasure his features could radiate. 'That's why I had the search warrant out for you. I had to know. And . . .' his eyes twinkled mischievously, 'we're due in Paris on Wednesday. I thought you might want a little time to prepare.'

'What?' Lynda gasped.

Paul chuckled. 'Don't look so appalled! It's a beautiful city, you know.'

'But what are we meant to go for?' Lynda didn't know whether she felt excited or dismayed.

Paul explained, 'Rees rang up last week and said there was a meeting of the consortium directors in Paris this Friday. Stately Homes is on the agenda for a final decision. He wants me to be there to explain the entire project again, in detail this time, to the group. And he expressly asked that you be there as well. Coming from Rees, that's an order.' He waited for her to respond.

'Well, aren't you pleased?'

Lynda considered before answering. She was secretly thrilled, flattered at the invitation. But she wasn't altogether prepared to let Paul see this. And she was nervous at the idea of more prolonged contact with him. He was looking at her expectantly.

'Yes, I am pleased,' she said calmly, 'but what will I have to do?'

'Just be prepared to talk about the project and go through your existing drawings with whoever's interested. It always helps when they can see things on paper. We can talk about the remaining houses now and over dinner, if you like.' He glanced down at his watch. 'Then you can make some more detailed notes on them tomorrow and tidy up these two drawings.'

Lynda got up to fetch a pad and pen.

'Let's talk now, but no dinner. I'm tired,' she said, making a feeble excuse.

He waited for her to sit down again before speaking. Then he gave her a long searching look. 'Lynda, you're not going to keep trying to avoid me, are you? I've taken the hint. I'll be on my best behaviour.'

She could feel her pulse beginning to race, the colour mounting to her cheeks. She avoided his gaze and shaking her head, said efficiently, 'Shall we begin?'

Paul's words brought the remaining houses in the project to life. Lynda asked questions and took copious notes. Then they went over to the drawings. When they had finished, Paul turned to her.

'Don't be offended, Lynda, but you will need some clothes. It's—well, it's the way things are in these circles. I'll lend you the money, if you don't have it on hand.'

She flushed, remembering the way she had flung the results of their last shopping spree in his face. 'Don't worry, I won't put you to shame. And I can afford a little more now,' she added, suddenly remembering her father's legacy. Her hand moved involuntarily to her locket, and Paul eyed her curiously.

'You've got something new around your neck.' He moved to touch the ring and she pulled away as if his fingers were fire. 'A ring,' he said suspiciously. 'Your mother's?' She shook her head and offered no further explanation.

'I see. So that's it.' He stood up to his full height and put out his hand rigidly. 'Should I extend my congratulations?'

Lynda got up too, ignoring his gesture. 'We're finished now, aren't we?' she said simply. She could see him trying to control his anger as he pulled his jacket brusquely over his broad shoulders.

Then he turned the full force of his eyes on her. 'I'll pick you up at four on Wednesday. Don't do a vanishing act again.' He thrust a cigarette into his mouth and with no further word turned to go. As he let himself out the door, she heard him greeting Tricia.

Tricia walked in shaking her head and threw her bag on the sofa. 'What's up between you two? He's been growling at me like some ferocious bear urging me to search for you, and now that you're here, he seems no happier. Couldn't you manage to placate him a little. He's making everyone's life miserable.' The words came out of her in a rush. 'And why didn't you tell me where you were going?'

Tricia stopped herself abruptly, 'Sorry, I haven't said welcome back yet. I'm a wreck!' She came to give Lynda a hug.

Lynda hugged her warmly in return, genuinely happy to see her again.

'I had no idea anyone would want me, and somehow I just assumed that you knew where I was going.'

'Well, you said home in your note, but I had to rack my brains to think where that might be. I finally remembered something that David had said and just hoped the telegram would reach you . . . What's it all about anyway? His arrogant highness didn't say.'

'We have to go to Paris on Wednesday for a meeting.'

Tricia looked at her in amazement. 'Why the glum faces all around, then?'

Lynda shrugged. 'I don't know. I guess I said the wrong thing.' Remembering, she raised her hand to her throat.

'Something significant?' Tricia queried as she caught sight of the ring.

Lynda didn't quite know what to say. It was difficult to put the truth simply and she wasn't altogether sure what the truth was. 'It's from David,' she offered. 'A sign of our continuing friendship.'

'Nothing more?' Tricia looked at her sceptically.

'Perhaps something more. We don't know yet.'

Tricia whistled softly through her teeth. 'You don't know when you're lucky!' She groped in her bag and pulled out her hairbrush, passing it through her long silky hair.

'You look well,' she said, eyeing Lynda up and down. 'The break has done you good. Are you going to get some new clothes for Paris?'

Lynda nodded. 'Boss's orders,' she added wryly.

Tricia chuckled, 'Well, he's so carelessly elegant himself, you don't want to put him to shame.'

Lynda flushed.

'Oh, I didn't mean it like that,' Tricia rushed to say. 'You're quite lovely enough for anyone. It's just that . . . well, Paris!' She walked across the room, mimicking a model's exaggerated gait.

Lynda laughed. 'You look wonderful! You've missed your calling.'

'I've done it, you know, but I gave it up—couldn't stand the people,' Tricia grimaced. 'Here, let me give you the address of the shop I go to. It's good and quite inexpensive.' She wrote a name down on a piece of paper and handed it to Lynda. 'Shall we have some food? I'm starved!'

Lynda nodded.

As the two girls sat down to table, Tricia said, 'Listen, Lynda, I've got something to confess to you. I've been meaning to tell you, but I haven't quite known how. Now that you and David—well . . .' she looked meaningfully at Lynda's ring, 'it's easier.'

Lynda looked at her expectantly.

'Robert and I have started up again.' Tricia seemed to be waiting for a reaction, but Lynda said nothing. She continued, a little hesitantly, 'It happened that weekend when you stood him up. We went out together and talked . . . talked about our rupture, about the child that I'd wanted and thought I had.'

'Oh, Tricia, how painful!' Lynda blurted out.

'Yes, it was rather.' Tricia smiled ironically as if she were gazing back at a distant self. 'But, in any case, that's in the past, a past full of misunderstandings. Anyhow, we've sort of patched things up now.'

Lynda couldn't stop a look of surprise coming to her face.

'Yes, I know, it's a little sudden. And he still makes up to everyone, if that's what you're thinking. It was one of the problems in the first place. But I've decided that's his way. Part of it is just his natural ebullience, and kindness.' She looked at Lynda intently, a little suspiciously.

'Oh, I am *glad*,' said Lynda, realising that she fully meant it. 'And the two of you look wonderful together.' She suddenly remembered Robert's distress that evening he had taken her out and had not wanted to talk about himself and Tricia. 'I think he does love you.'

It was Tricia's turn to shrug. 'Well, we'll see how long it lasts this time. He's not altogether to be trusted.'

They looked at each other and both burst out laughing, saying in unison, 'Men are just not to be trusted!'

The next morning Lynda woke with a sense of excitement. Tomorrow she would be going to Paris. And she would enjoy every moment, despite Paul, she determined. But there was so much to do first. She threw on some clothes, drank a quick cup of coffee and sat down at her desk to make the drawing alterations Paul had suggested. Then she rushed to the office to type up notes on the remaining house interiors. As she went up in the lift, she resolved to keep a professional mask on where Paul was concerned and hold her emotions on a tight rein. She practised a swift bright smile and pushed her hair back from her face.

Pleased with herself, she walked into the office. Paul for once was sitting at his desk, his head buried in plans. Lynda thrust the portfolio of drawings on his desk and with the bright smile uttered a crisp 'Good Morning' and strode off. He looked at her unseeingly and muttered a greeting in return.

A few moments later she could sense him coming up to her. She braced herself and looked up with the same bright smile.

'Are the drawings all right?' she queried coolly.

He gave her a long look from beneath thick lashes and then answered in the same tone of voice.

'They seem all right. I just wanted to tell you that I've instructed Cindy to type up the notes when they're done. I'll pick them up from her tomorrow and go over them.'

Lynda nodded her thanks and turned her face back down to her desk. Paul stood above her for a moment. She felt he wanted to say something more, but she didn't allow herself to look up at him. Finally, he walked off saying, 'I'll see you tomorrow.'

Lynda breathed a sigh of relief. It wasn't so bad. If she could keep that up, it would just about be possible to see the whole thing through.

She worked without a break until she had finished the notes and only then looked at her watch. It was almost four. If she was to go to the shop Tricia had recommended, she would have to hurry.

The boutique turned out to be a small one run by a tiny but exquisite Frenchwoman who seemed prepared to offer advice or not—as the customer preferred. Lynda explained that she wasn't altogether sure what she wanted, but—she was surprised to hear herself saying all this—she was going to Paris and she wanted something that would travel well. The woman looked her up and down, walked to the rear of the shop and came back with a beautifully tailored cream-coloured woollen suit.

'How about this?' she asked in her slightly accented English.

Lynda slipped the straight skirt on. It fitted perfectly, moulding her hips just a little. Small slits on either side made walking comfortable. She was about to try on the jacket when the woman passed a striped cream and black silky shirt through the dressing-room curtain.

'This would go very well with it,' she suggested.

Lynda gazed at her reflection in the mirror-covered wall at the back of the shop.

'Perfect, my dear. You look stunningly elegant,' the manageress said as she adjusted the wide belt around Lynda's slender waist. 'Now try this with it.' She reached for a soft felt broad-brimmed hat and handed it to Lynda.

'Oh, I couldn't!'

'Why not? Here, let me do it for you.' She placed the hat at a slightly rakish tilt on Lynda's head and played with the brim, looking at her with her head to one side. 'It would be better still if you put your hair up.' With one sure gesture, she coiled Lynda's hair and tucked it under the hat. 'There! You look as if you've walked straight out of the pages of *Vogue*.'

A quick look in the mirror reassured Lynda. She looked poised, coolly sophisticated. Paul would be aghast. She flashed the quick bright smile she had practised into the mirror and said, 'I'll take it . . . all.'

She didn't dare ask the price, but when the woman asked her whether she'd like to see anything else, she voiced her misgivings.

'I did want a dress as well, but I don't think I could afford one on top of this.'

'Let me tempt you with something inexpensive,' the woman looked at her maternally. 'I like my customers to come back!'

She brought out two dresses for Lynda to look at. One was a softly feminine terra-cotta jersey with a tiny waist and loosely-gathered flowing skirt. Its delicate scalloped collar ended just short of a demure V-shaped neckline. The other was a slightly more extravagant affair of deep blue crêpe-de-chine with widely flowing sleeves which then deceptively finished in a tight band around the wrist.

Lynda tried both and was helpless to choose.

'Take both, my dear. You look so well in them.'

Lynda finally dared to ask what the bill would come to. Tricia had been right; the prices were quite reasonable.

Why not? she thought to herself. I won't be going to Paris again in a hurry. And then, as if apologising to her mother, I haven't bought any clothes in donkey's years.

She walked out of the shop swinging her various bags and feeling altogether elated.

Tricia was just walking in the front door when Lynda arrived home.

'You've done well, by the look of things,' she said, taking in Lynda's various packages.

'I'm afraid I've been terribly extravagant,' Lynda beamed happily. 'Wait till you see it all!' They hurried upstairs and before Tricia had had a chance to take her jacket off, Lynda displayed her various purchases.

'Wonderful! Did Madame Buffet help you, the small dark Frenchwoman? I think I can detect her hand in all this.'

Lynda nodded.

'She's quite amazing. She used to work for an haute couture boutique before she came to London. Go on, try them on for me.'

Lynda did, and Tricia murmured her enthusiasm. 'You'll wow the Frenchmen,' she said wryly.

Lynda wasn't sure about the Frenchmen, but certainly Paul's look of frank admiration when he came to pick her up promptly at four the next day rid her of any qualms she might have had. As she adjusted the new hat over her freshly washed coiled hair, and turned to face him, he murmured, 'Perfect! Too good, in fact. I'll have to beat Rees away from you.' He chuckled as she coloured slightly and reached for her travel bag. He took it from her, squeezing her hand in passing. Then he met her eyes and gave her a long warm smile.

'Shall we try to be amicable, Lynda? I do promise to be on my best behaviour.'

She returned his look and nodded, made a little breathless by the rugged beauty of his face when he determined to be charming.

Paul seemed to be in rare good humour as they drove to the airport, and she soon learned the secret of it.

'If these meetings go well—and with you looking as you do, we can't go wrong,' he murmured a joking aside, 'the project's sewn up. Two years of preliminary work and battling finished with. And at last, we can get on to the real thing—the houses. Rees on the telephone promised support, so we're eighty per cent there ... .'

Lynda suddenly realised the pressure Paul must have been under all this time. He had always seemed so sure, so confident, it had never occurred to her that he might be deeply worried, that all the energy he had invested in the project might come to nothing. She suddenly felt petty, childish. No wonder he had berated her about her lack of professionalism!

'I'll help all I can,' she said with feeling.

He glanced at her briefly, surprised at the warmth in her tone.

'And I'm not,' he emphasised it, 'asking you to sell yourself.'

They arrived at the airport in good time and in high spirits. Paul parked the car and a little shuttle bus took them to their terminal.

'Plenty of time for a drink,' he said, ushering her towards a corner seat and then moving off towards the bar. He seemed to know the terminal inside out. Lynda, as she watched him returning with the drinks, drew in a sharp breath. He walked with the grace of a cat, effortlessly covering the space between them. She saw women, looking up to watch him, the movement of his broad shoulders encased in the tawny leather jacket she so liked, his trim waist, the long tweed-clad legs. It came to her that she was very fortunate to be in the company of such a man.

He handed her her drink and sat down beside her. She moved her eyes into the vague distance, unable to trust herself to meet his.

'Do you travel much?' she asked, working to keep her voice steady.

'Too much,' he chuckled, 'but I'm still thrilled by it. Every time I get into an aeroplane, I feel I'm in a special capsule, quite shielded from time. And you?'

She hesitated to say it. It would only be the second time she had ever flown. The first had been on a college trip when a group of students had been taken to Rome to look at paintings. She shook her head.

'Well, I hope it's a good flight. It will be brief in any case. Do you know Paris well?'

This time she laughed. 'I've only been once— when I was twelve, on a school trip. We took the ferry from Dover.'

'I can show you the sights, then,' he chuckled, 'between work hours, that is.'

Their flight was called and he took her arm and led her towards their gate. The stewardess, eyeing Paul admiringly, guided them towards their seats.

'I thought that since we had important business to attend to this evening, we'd travel first class,' Paul said, winking at Lynda as he made room for her to move into the window seat.

'Business?' she asked, stiffening slightly.

He chuckled again. 'Don't panic! Rees is coming to have dinner with us to brief us on the state of affairs. Or perhaps just to have a look at his favourite Englishwoman.'

Lynda flushed and played with her seat-belt, unable to do the clasp in her nervousness.

'Here, let me help.' He reached over to fasten it for her, his long fingers trailing over her thighs as he did so. She shuddered slightly. Then, remembering her resolve to be coolly poised, she thanked him, removed her hat and turned her flushed face towards the window.

London receded beneath them. Lynda's excitement mounted with the plane's ascent. She closed her eyes, imagining what she remembered of Paris, the regal boulevards, the cobbled climbing streets of Montmartre.

Suddenly she felt a pair of lips coolly brushing her cheeks. She opened her eyes wide and let out an involuntary gasp.

'Sorry. I can't resist sleeping women,' Paul murmured in her ear, his tone still half-jocular.

'And I can't resist men when I'm asleep,' she found herself retorting, not realising quite what she had said until it was out.

Paul looked at her unnervingly for a brief moment, and then with steady coolness said, 'I'll have to see you more often when you're asleep then.'

The stewardess saved her from having to reply by offering drinks. Before Lynda had quite finished hers, the seat-belt and No Smoking sign lit up. She pulled her hat on, trying to glimpse a reflection of herself in the darkening window.

They landed smoothly in Charles de Gaulle airport. Lynda was thrilled by the giant bubble with its intimate corners and maze of space fiction escalators. She almost forgot Paul's presence at her side until she heard him telling her a story about the aeroport's architect. She tried not to let her little girl amazement show too much as she followed him towards the taxi exit.

'We'll take a cab,' he said, 'otherwise there won't be time to settle in before Rees arrives.'

As she heard Paul giving instructions to the driver, Lynda was amazed at the faultless fluency of his French.

'Where did you learn that?' she queried, hoping the driver wouldn't hear.

He shrugged. 'I lived here for a while, but then I can't remember ever not speaking French. How about you?'

'Faltering schoolgirl variety, and God knows if I even remember that,' Lynda grimaced. A worry occurred to her. 'Will the meeting take place in French?'

'Partly, I imagine. But don't worry, it will all be translated if necessary. Shaw always thinks he's missing some cagey detail, though his French is quite good enough.'

The taxi took them over the Seine, its waters swift and silvery in the fading pink light of the setting sun. Lynda tingled with excitement as the beauty of the city came home to her. To her left, the intricate façade of Notre-Dame reached towards the sky; to her right, graceful bridges arched the curves of the river. She breathed a sigh of pure pleasure.

Paul reached for her hand and squeezed it.

Unaware, she returned the pressure of his fingers.

'The beauty of it all never ceases to amaze me,' he said quietly, and Lynda nodded agreement, her eyes glowing.

They pulled up in front of a small hotel on one of the narrow streets which wound its way south from the river into the Latin Quarter, rue des Saints-Pères. The street of the saintly fathers, Lynda translated freely, and smiled wryly to herself, thinking of her own saintly father.

The hotel had a discreet air. Its milky white façade blended unobtrusively with those of the antique shops, galleries, and boutiques which surrounded it. Yet its blue plaque bore four stars, and as its doors were opened for them, she could see why. The hushed interior was a model of quiet elegance. The intimacy of the softly lit lobby gave way into a glass-covered courtyard where plants burgeoned around small tables. Amidst the muted voices, she could hear the receptionist welcoming Paul warmly by name and then the cultivated resonance of Paul's voice. A strange ache drew her towards him.

As she approached, he turned. Their eyes met with a searing intensity which made them both look away. Paul introduced her to Monsieur Verdoux, the manager, as *'ma collègue'*, my colleague. Lynda felt flattered at the description and she brought out her best, *'Enchantée, monsieur,'* as she shook the manager's outstretched hand. She noticed a brief approving look passing between him and Paul. It gave her an added confidence as she followed the dark-eyed attendant towards the lift.

Their rooms were on the top floor, rooms which, as Lynda later discovered, were regularly reserved for Paul. She gasped with delight when she saw hers—a bed, covered in lush Bordeaux satin, a small

walnut secretaire and dressing table, two well-cush-
ioned armchairs positioned around a circular coffee
table, and best of all, large French windows opening
on to a small terrace from which one could see the
river and the cathedral of Notre-Dame. The walls
were papered in a delicate cream embossed with
silver stripes and tiny fleur-de-lys. The bathroom,
Lynda noted with relief, had no adjoining door and
all the amenities associated with the privileged
French toilette, numerous thick towels, scented soap,
a beautiful oval-shaped mirror, a marble floor,
ornate tap fittings.

'I could stay here for ever,' she whispered to
Paul.

He smiled at her delight.

'You take your time and enjoy it. I'll meet you at
the bar in a little while.'

He closed the door quietly behind him. Lynda
arranged her clothes and then was unable to resist
going out on the terrace. The city stretched before
her in the dusky light, roofs playfully edging into
one another following the shapes of the streets. Notre
Dame, now illuminated, looked even grander.
Twinkling lights bounced off the waters of the Seine.
Lynda stood there lost in time and then mentally
pinched herself. She must get ready for dinner.

It was too late to shower, but she did want to
change, so she washed quickly and considered her
new clothes. She decided on the blue crêpe-de-chine.
The way its loosely gathered skirt and flowing sleeves
caught the light and reflected it, its rustling sound as
she moved, made Lynda feel quite extraordinarily
glamorous. She made up her eyes with a luminescent
blue and added a hint of sparkle to her lips. Then,
carrying Tricia's loose wrap over her arm, she made
her way to the lift. She felt ready for anything.

CHAPTER EIGHT

In her best French Lynda asked the receptionist the
way to the bar and he pointed her in the proper
direction. She entered a darkly-lit room. It took a
few moments for her eyes to accustom themselves to
the dimness. Then she made out Stanford Rees and
Paul sitting in a corner, deep in conversation. They
didn't notice her, and in those few unobserved
seconds she indulged herself in the sight of Paul, his
brow furrowed in concentration, the straight pure
line of his Grecian nose. He looked devastating in a
dark charcoal suit, deep blue shirt and loosely
knotted crimson tie. How could she protect herself
against his vitality?

Suddenly he spotted her and rose. She was grateful
for the half light which hid her embarrassment as
she walked towards their table, her silky dress
caressing her legs. Stanford Rees rose too and moved
forward to meet her. He embraced her and kissed
her on both cheeks, whispering into her ear, 'When
in France . . .'

She laughed, finding herself very glad indeed to
see him, the curly mass of salt and pepper hair, the
odour of pipe tobacco about his clothes, the crisp
tones of his mid-Atlantic English.

'You look even more ravishing than I remember,'
he said, and she heard Paul drawl almost inaudibly,
'if not ravishable.'

The two men were drinking tall glasses of a pale
milky-yellow liquid.

'Can I get you a Pernod?' Stanford Rees offered.

'Or something else?'

'A Pernod, please,' said Lynda, the word sounding glamorous on her tongue. She gave him a deliberately wide-eyed look and whispered conspiratorially, 'I've never had one.'

He chuckled. 'An authentic English hick we've got here, Overton,' and as he sensed Lynda bristling, added seriously, 'Wish I were one still. It allows you to enjoy things all the more!'

The slender moustachioed waiter placed a glass of colourless liquid in front of Lynda and poured some water into it. The glass turned milky yellow. She sipped the heavily scented drink and made a funny face. 'Liquorice,' she said.

'Anise,' Paul corrected her. 'Pernod is the legitimate offspring of Absinthe. Remember those early Picassos and the pale green glass in front of the cadaverous figures? When all of Paris was drinking it at the turn of the century, the poets and bohemians dubbed seven o'clock, the green hour. I've never been too sure whether it was to do with the colour of the drink or the haze through which you saw life afterwards. Luckily, Pernod doesn't have the same corrosive effect on the brain . . . or my trips to France would be numbered,' he laughed, taking a large sip from his glass.

'It grows on you,' said Lynda, joining him.

'Not too fast, I hope,' Stanford Rees quipped. 'I want to take you out of here to one of my favourite restaurants. I've booked a table for us.'

The restaurant was only a few minutes away on the Quai Voltaire, overlooking the Seine, and they walked the distance through the crisp, clear night air. It occupied the top floor of a corner building. Two of its walls were glass and offered a breathtaking view of Paris. It was strangely like being both in the sky and on the river at the same time.

Lynda felt herself floating, slightly giddy from the drink and from the many excitements of the day. Her eyes sparkled as she sat down between the two handsome men at a table covered in brilliant white and heavy silver. She couldn't quite believe it was she who was sitting here.

Paul leaned towards her to help her with the menu's French. His nearness made her pulse quicken and on an impulse she let her hand brush his. He looked at her intently, questioningly and, colouring, she drew away and turned towards Stanford.

'I feel like Cinderella. Do you think all this will vanish at midnight?' She swept the room with her gaze.

'Not a chance, young lady. It's been here for over a hundred years. And I'll keep a firm grip on you so you don't vanish before the meeting either.' He took hold of her hand to emphasise his words.

Out of the corner of her eye, Lynda could see Paul's face darkening, but he simply cleared his throat and said in a husky voice, 'Shall we order now?'

Stanford nodded and Lynda buried her face in the menu. There was simply too much to choose from and she felt greedily that she wanted it all. She voiced her plight.

Paul laughed. 'We'll both let you taste all of ours, but why don't you start with some escargots, in garlic butter?'

'And the tournedos here is marvellous,' Stanford suggested. 'There's nothing comparable in England, if I remember.'

'It all sounds wonderful,' Lynda murmured.

Stanford ordered a bottle of champagne to set the mood and then discussed the menu in detail with the waiter. The two men seemed equally versed in the intricacies of sauces and seasonings, and Lynda was content to let them get on with it while she allowed the dry bubbly champagne to tickle her nose.

The waiter, immaculate in tails and starched white, served the various courses, brought dishes filled with terrine, moules, escargots, then gigots and tournedos cooked to perfection, potato croquettes, buttered spinach, endive and scarole salad. Meanwhile conversation flowed, randomly, gaily.

By the time Lynda bit into the delectable tiny wild strawberries and crumbly pastry of her sweet, the world had been transformed into a rosy, trouble-free spectacle. The mellow but inaudible tones of *La Vie en Rose* filled her ears.

She leaned carelessly, lightly against Paul as they walked back to the hotel, matching her steps exactly to his. At the door, Stanford kissed her on both cheeks.

'Make sure you're in top form tomorrow evening when we meet the French crew,' he said to her. And shaking hands with Paul, he added, 'Take good care of our young lady.'

As if obeying an order, Paul put his arm protectively around her and guided her into the hotel. She glided along beside him, thrilled by the sense of his hard body against hers. In the solitude of the lift, she lifted her eyes to his and met their full impact.

Then abruptly Paul withdrew his eyes, his arm, his body. A chill shook her, a coldness which pervaded her every fibre. She forced herself to walk out of the lift, to move her legs towards her room. At her door, Paul murmured, his voice rough with an edge of anger, 'If you behave like that, I can't gua-rantee that you'll spend your nights alone—I'm not made of steel. Goodnight.' He turned on his heel and strode off swiftly.

Lynda wanted to run after him, to entreat him, but her feet refused to move. After what seemed an eternity, she put her key into the lock and let herself into the room. Without turning on a light she sat at the edge of the bed, numbed by her conflicting emotions. One part of her mind listened for movements from the room next door. Suddenly she made out the sound of a door closing. She listened breathlessly, half hoping that the footsteps would stop at her door. But they moved softly down the corridor and away without stopping.

She paced round her room, an abyss opening at the pit of her stomach. Not altogether aware of her actions, she made her way downstairs. Like a sleepwalker she moved towards the bar and entered it.

What she saw bolted her into wakefulness. There sat Paul with a beautifully groomed dark-haired woman. She was gazing at him with sultry eyes as he stroked her hand rhythmically. Obviously not a recent acquaintance, Lynda thought bitterly. She turned and ran, almost knocking over the man behind her.

In her room, she tore off her clothes and lay naked on the bed staring at the intricate mouldings in the ceiling. I have no right to feel like this, I have no right to feel like this, she repeated to herself ceaselessly, trying to stay her mounting jealousy. And if I'd wanted to be with him now, I could have been. She was by now quite sure of that. Yet the thought did occur to her that Paul's nocturnal meeting must have been prearranged.

She got up to douse herself with cold water. I don't care, was her last waking thought. I don't want to be just another meaningless fling away from Vanessa.

The morning dawned bright and clear. Standing out on the terrace, Lynda let the magic of the city still her fraught emotions. A knock at the door brought in a pretty maid who explained that Monsieur had left instructions that breakfast was to be brought up to the room.

Lynda broke off a piece of the flaky croissant, dunked it in her café-au-lait and savoured the taste. She considered: she had promised herself that she would enjoy this trip, not allow herself to be affected by Paul and already she had broken her vow. It was madness to feel miserable amidst all this beauty . . . and for a man who couldn't care less about her to boot. She looked out on the buttresses and spires of Notre-Dame and repeated her vow. 'After all, two can play at this game,' she said aloud, defying the spires and not altogether sure what she meant by it.

She dressed hurriedly. Paul had told her he had business to attend to in the morning (Some business! she now scoffed) and would meet her for lunch. Well, she wouldn't waste a second of the morning. She strode through the lobby and out on to the street, only to find herself being called.

'Mademoiselle, Mademoiselle!' the receptionist hailed her, and gave her an envelope. Lynda tore it open, a little surprised. It contained a brief note from Paul saying he hoped she had slept well and giving the address of the restaurant they would meet in at one. He had drawn her a detailed map.

Lynda smiled. Obviously he didn't want her to stray away altogether.

She walked along the narrow streets of the Latin Quarter, browsing through numerous art galleries and bookshops, gazing longingly into the many boutiques displaying sometimes outlandish, sometimes classical fashions. As she stared into one, she saw Paul's reflection walking towards her, next to him the woman she seemed to recognise from yesterday evening. She veered round impulsively to look over the road, but a van was passing and by the time it had moved away, they seemed to have disappeared.

Lynda crossed the street to look into the shop she was certain she had seen them emerging from. It was a boutique filled with delicate lingerie and on a whim she went in and began fingering the satin negligees and silk petticoats. She saw a beautiful pair of oyster pink silk camiknickers, delicately embroidered with hearts and flowers and trimmed with soft lace, and still on a whim and feeling decidedly naughty, she bought them. Why not? she thought to herself. Perhaps I can charge *these* to expenses!

The sheer wickedness of the thought gave her pleasure and she smiled widely as she handed the money over to the shop attendant. Turning the corner where she thought Paul must have gone, she found herself in a market street. Barrows full of wonderfully displayed fruit and vegetables jostled with flower merchants, butchers and bakers. It all made her desperately hungry and she walked into a boulangerie to buy one of those chocolate-filled pastries which she remembered nostalgically from her girlhood.

Munching away, she glanced at her watch and realised she only had fifteen minutes in which to get to the restaurant. No time to change. She reached for the map Paul had drawn, got her bearings and breathed a sigh of relief. The restaurant was just at the other end of the Boulevard St Germain.

She walked briskly and arrived at the brasserie only a few minutes late. She looked round, but there was no sight of Paul in the glassed-in terrasse. She found him sitting at a back table, his face buried in a French newspaper and sipping a drink.

'Hello,' he looked up at her and smiled. 'Have a good morning?'

'Wonderful,' Lynda nodded, crossing one long leg over another and leaning back into a chair. 'But I'm exhausted.'

'Drink? Campari and soda?'

She nodded again and placed the bag from the lingerie shop conspicuously on the table. He glanced at it and she thought she could detect a hint of embarrassment in his face.

Lynda looked up at him provocatively. 'You look pretty tired. Hard night?'

His blue eyes glinted and the gracious smile left his face. But he didn't take her up on it. Instead, he turned to catch the waiter's eye.

'What are the plans for today?' she asked, taking a long sip of the bittersweet drink.

'I thought I'd brief you over lunch on the various people we're to see. Then, if there's time, we could catch the Picasso retrospective before going on to Debray's at six.'

'You don't have to take me round, you know, if you have better things to do.'

He took a long puff of his cigarette. 'If I felt I had *better* things to do, Lynda Harrow,' his tone was scathing and he separated the syllables in her name as he had done when they first met, 'I would do them. So stop taunting me.' His eyes flashed.

She glanced at him archly and then burst into a giggle.

He looked nonplussed.

'Sorry,' she said trying to stop her laughter. 'It's just that . . . well, you have this wonderful way of speaking when you're angry. I think I'm be-

Paul's stunned silence when he had seen her enter the hotel lobby had made it all worthwhile. Looking her up and down, he had reached protectively for her arm. 'I shall have to work hard to defend you from the wolves,' he had said.

And he had not been wrong, she realised now as she felt the gaze of several pairs of male eyes on her in Monsieur Debray's large delicately gilded drawing-room. It was almost as if the only thing which remained between her and stark nudity were her new camiknickers.

Monsieur Debray, a suave man with iron-grey hair and piercing eyes beneath a prominent brow, shook her hand warmly and murmured an emphatic, '*Enchanté*, Mademoiselle Harrow. Mr Rees has spoken to me of you.' Then turning to Paul, he said with a hint of irony, 'Your Mr Dunlop seems to choose his staff with an eye to *structure*, *n'est-ce pas*?'

'And to talent,' she heard Paul reply in deep tones as she turned to greet Stanford Rees, who kissed her companionably and murmured, 'I think I *will* take you back to America with me.'

She smiled. Monsieur Debray led her and Paul away to meet his wife, a tall elegant woman clothed in black with black hair drawn softly back from a strong-featured face. She had a remote air about her, as if she would much rather be alone in her room than in this company, but she welcomed Lynda politely in perfect English.

Then Lynda found herself looking into satin-dark eyes in a deeply bronzed face and being greeted by a flash of perfect white teeth.

'My son and partner, Claude,' Monsieur Debray said. 'I shall leave him to introduce you to the others.'

Lynda was startled. She had been told nothing of a son, and certainly nothing of a son like this. Claude was almost too perfect, his trim body clad in a satin-lapelled dinner jacket over a silky white shirt open at the neck to give the whole a casual air.

'I thought this was going to be a dull business dinner, but I was obviously mistaken,' he said in French, turning the full attention of his good looks on her. 'You do speak French?' he queried.

'A little. A little more if you speak slowly.'

He smiled at her, his dark eyes crinkling with charm as he handed her a drink from the tray the maid had brought round. 'I suppose I have to introduce you to the others, but then I shall steal you for myself.'

He presented her to a tall, gleamingly bald-headed German with a ferocious tilt to his nose, Herr Spengler; and to a round jocular Frenchman, the incarnation of a *bon-vivant*, and his daintily pretty wife, Monsieur and Madame Resnais. Then she spied Northrop Shaw, who had just entered the room, and went to greet him. It seemed this was the sum total of the party. She noticed Paul in animated conversation with Monsieur Debray, so she followed Claude to a quiet corner of the room.

They were still talking when dinner was announced. At the long, highly polished dining table, Lynda found herself between Stanford and Claude, both of whom showered her with attention and vied for her conversation. By the time they had reached the main course, a delicately-sauced quail on a bed of wild rice, she was quipping gaily with both of them. Flushed and warmed by the seemingly endless succession of wines, she moved to take off her jacket, something she hadn't quite dared to do before. Claude reached to help and handed it to the maid.

Suddenly Lynda caught an angry glare from Paul, sitting at the opposite end of the table. She automatically crossed her arms to cover her exposed shoulders with her hands. But then, thinking better of it, she smiled at him brazenly, lowered her arms slowly and turned to Claude. Two can play, old grump, she thought to herself.

After dinner Monsieur Debray took her off for a short chat. They were joined by the jocular Frenchman and the German. Little snippets of business talk were interspersed with more general conversation. Lynda felt she wasn't handling things too badly, but she was relieved when Claude came to draw her away.

'Perhaps you would like to go now and see a little of Parisian night life?' She was tempted, but the sight of Paul approaching them determinedly made her shake her head.

'Tomorrow, then, I could show you some sights and perhaps we could even take a little drive to our country house.'

Paul loomed behind him. 'Miss Harrow has a rather important meeting to attend tomorrow. It is in fact why she's here.' His tone was abrasive, and Lynda bristled.

'Perhaps I could give you a ring after the meeting,' she said, looking at Claude archly.

'Wonderful, I'll get you my number.'

As Claude went in search of his card, Paul gripped her arm fiercely. She remembered the pressure of that grip and shivered imperceptibly. He manoeuvred her towards their host.

'It's time we left. I want you awake for that meeting tomorrow.'

She wrenched her arm away from him. 'You're hurting me!' She looked up into the blackness of his eyes, dizzied by the rage she read there. Then she turned to try and smile politely and offer thanks to their host.

As they walked towards the door, Claude handed her his card and uttered a low, 'Until tomorrow, then.'

Lynda smiled and nodded.

The gate had only just shut behind them when Paul gripped her arm again.

'Enjoy yourself flirting outrageously with that coxcomb?'

'More than I enjoy you growling at me,' she parried.

Brusquely he let go of her arm. There was silence between them as they walked, Lynda almost running to keep up with his long strides.

When they came to a main road, Paul hailed a taxi. Still he said nothing to her. They sat at opposite ends of the seat, both looking out of their windows. She felt desolate in her separateness.

Suddenly she sensed him moving towards her, felt an arm weave its way round her waist, a mouth searching hungrily for hers. She trembled and met his lips. Their heat scalded every pore in her body, making her limply tremulous. He buried his face in her hair.

'If you're going to flirt with anyone, it's going to be me,' she heard him say as if from a great distance.

With no awareness of how she had got there, Lynda found herself in Paul's room at the hotel. She was standing on the terrace looking out on the twinkling lights of the city and balancing a glass of champagne which had miraculously appeared in her hand. From somewhere below came the pulsing strains of a jazz guitar.

She sensed Paul behind her, felt the caress of his fingertips as he took the glass from her hand. A second later he was behind her again, his long arms encircling her waist, his strong fingers gently stroking the rise of her satin-clad bosom. She felt her limbs turning liquid, incapable of movement.

He pressed his taut body firmly to hers, moulding his shape against her. His breath echoed in her ear. Above it, she could just make out a hoarse murmur, 'Beautiful, so beautiful.'

She swayed helplessly against him. He lifted her gently, tenderly in his arms and carried her into the dim light of the room. As if remembering her fear of the bed, he led them to the deep velvet armchair. She snuggled into his lap, curling her face against his chest, afraid to look at him.

He urged her face to his and looked deeply into her eyes, and she was frightened of the smouldering passion she read on his face. But before she could turn away, he pressed his lips to hers, first softly, then with an increasing intensity. She responded, unable to resist, found her arms enfolding his broad back, her fingers stroking the thick electric hair she had so often wanted to touch.

Paul uttered a low moan and moved his head to follow her touch.

'I've dreamt of you doing that,' he said huskily, almost inaudibly, and brought his mouth down on hers with a new pressure. She shuddered with a pleasure which seemed to tense each part of her body. Her skin grew almost painfully sensitive to his touch.

With one expert movement he released her halter top and moved his lips down the length of her neck to her bosom. She arched her body to meet the descent of his lips, each pore thrilling at the stroke of his hand.

But as his fingers began to caress her stomach, reaching below the satin of her trousers, Lynda's mind suddenly came to life and she stopped his hand.

He looked into her eyes, his face so utterly beautiful in its mixture of concern and desire that she felt her breath stop.

'What is it, Lynda? You do want me, don't you? Are you . . . is it the first time?' he asked in a voice husky with tenderness.

She felt half tempted to shake her head, to throw over this burden of virginity.

He watched her silence attentively.

'I won't hurt you,' he said in a whisper, stroking the length of her thigh. 'I'll be gentle, very gentle.' He enveloped her hand in his and pressed a searching kiss on her lips, and she opened to him.

But suddenly she shuddered and pushing him away, jumped up. Her mind's eye had presented her with a full-blown picture of Vanessa slithering over the television screen and then with equal suddenness an image of the dark woman she had seen with Paul. Instinctively her hand reached to touch her mother's locket.

'So that's it,' he said, misinterpreting her gesture, his eyes blazing. He towered to his full height, and looked down on her with scathing contempt. 'It's a little late in the day to play faithful Miss. And if you're going to, don't go around taunting everyone like a brazen hussy!' He brought the last two words out with a cutting clarity, throwing her jacket at her and turning his back to face the terrace.

Lynda gazed at his broad shoulders in dismay, searching vainly for her tongue. But then anger at his sudden brutality stirred her.

'And what about your own fidelity, then, Mr

Architect Overton? I don't really care for one-night stands with other women's men!' She brought it out slowly, waiting until he turned to look at her, and then slamming the door behind her as he moved to answer.

CHAPTER NINE

LYNDA paced her room, her blood boiling, unable to calm herself enough to sit or lie down. Then she heard Paul's door slamming and his feet walking determinedly down the corridor.

'The rat!' she exclaimed out loud, and then as she remembered the mingled force and tenderness of his passion, she burst into tears.

Huddled into her pillow, she cried for a long time. Self-pity, anger, self-contempt, and then finally a pure longing took their turns in her. I should have taken up Claude's offer and avoided all this, she thought to herself at last as she looked at her watch through tear-stained eyes.

It was two in the morning and tomorrow was a working day. She went to stand in the shower, letting the strong stream of water wash the tension from her skin.

I'll never be able to face him now, was the thought on which she finally closed her eyes.

The next morning she woke early and dressed hurriedly in her new terra-cotta dress. She left her room quietly, hoping to avoid Paul, and went to a café to drink a morning coffee and gaze mournfully at the Seine.

A soft mist was rising from the waters. The streets looked freshly washed. There was an unnatural stillness about everything, broken only by the revving of an occasional car or the clackety-clack of a woman's high-heeled shoes along the pavement.

Each sound distinct.

Lynda glanced at her watch. It was only seven-thirty. The meeting was scheduled for ten. She ordered another café-au-lait, munched half heartedly at a jam-laden tartine and tried to look at her situation coolly.

She couldn't avoid the meeting; that would be professionally unethical. So she would have to see Paul. The very thought of his presence suddenly overwhelmed her. Her pulse throbbed with an alarming insistence and she could see her hands tremble visibly as she brought the cup to her lips.

She took a large gulp of the scalding liquid, and the tears rushed to her eyes, but she blinked them back.

'*Ça va, mademoiselle?* Are you all right?' The elderly waiter had caught her gesture. She tried a watery smile and nodded.

'*Ah, les chagrins d'amour!* Love problems, no?' He made a sad little pout with his mouth and then gave her a warm, flickering smile. 'He has left you, *hein*? But he will come back.' He moved to pat her hand gently. '*Tout s'arrange.* Everything will come right. You are so young, so charming. There, there, wipe your tears and give me a smile.'

Lynda suddenly realised that the tears had been flowing down her cheeks. She wiped them with a tissue she found in her bag and smiled at the old man.

'No, nothing will come right!' she wanted to shout. 'He won't come back, because he hasn't really been there in the first place.' But yes, she loved him— God, how she loved him! She wanted to run her fingers through his thick hair just once more, feel the weight of his body pressed against her. She shuddered.

What was the good of that? Yes, of course, she could have him, for a night, for two or three. His passion, she knew, had been real enough. But then, not to have him always, to know he was with, belonged to, another woman. No, she couldn't bear that, the pain of it. Better to go away, to forget.

She reached for her purse. Suddenly the waiter was by her side, holding out a fragrant white rose to her.

'For the melancholy young lady of the morning,' he said with an old-fashioned grace.

Lynda smiled her thanks and pulled the flower through a buttonhole on her dress.

She strolled away from the Seine along the narrow cobbled streets of St Germain. The shops were beginning to open and she paused for a moment in front of a tiny boutique, so small and so crowded with jewellery that there was almost no room for customers. Beautiful objects in silver crowded the window space, finely crafted antique pendants with flower-like ladies, bracelets alive with vines.

Looking at the tiny price tags, she realised that the jewellery must be reproduction and she went in. Yes, she would buy something for Tricia who had been so kind to her, and for her sisters.

Lynda chose the purchases with care. A heavy pendant with a graceful long-haired sylph for Tricia; a bracelet replete with tiny flowers for her sister Caroline; and a bird-shaped pin for Sarah. Then she spied a small ornate silver box. Its lid bore the image of a man, head thrown back, sitting at a piano. The energy of the music was visible in every indentation the jeweller's hand had made.

David, Lynda thought. I must get it for him. The price was far more than she could afford, but she must have it. On an impulse, she took his ring from the chain round her neck and placed it in the small box. Yes, that was right. She couldn't give David hope where there was none. She couldn't marry him feeling what she did for Paul—even if he only became a ghost flitting through the crevices of her memory.

She shivered slightly and again the tears leapt to her eyes. But she stilled them determinedly, asked the shop attendant if he could wrap the gifts separately and securely. Then she took a bit of notepaper from her bag and wrote a brief message to David. Better, she thought, to do this now, or I might weaken.

'David,' she wrote, 'it would be unfair for me to keep this, to pretend to hope. But please believe that I value our friendship above anything.' 'Yes, above anything,' she said out loud, as she folded the note into the cardboard box the attendant had given her. Then, asking for directions, she made her way to the nearest post office and posted the gifts, keeping only Tricia's behind.

The streets had now filled with people. Lynda glanced at her watch and saw it was time for the meeting. She hailed a taxi and tried to compose herself for the inevitable confrontation with Paul.

The taxi took her beyond the Eiffel Tower, over the Seine to a modern office block set well back from the street. Large contemporary sculptures decorated its grounds. She took the lift to the tenth floor and stepped out into a carpeted hall bounded on one side by ceiling-to-floor windows. The view was breathtaking and she paused for a moment to look out on the intricacy of Paris roofs, the graceful lines of the plane-tree-bordered streets.

When all's said and done, she thought to herself, I'm terribly lucky, and as the receptionist asked for her name, she plastered a wide smile on her face and gave it. Then she strode firmly into a long board-room, whose large windows now gave her a fresh aspect of the city.

Stanford Rees, Monsieur Debray and Northrop Shaw were already in the room and rose to greet her. They shook hands all round, slightly more formal today, in keeping with the atmosphere of the boardroom.

'The others should be here in a moment,' Monsieur Debray said to her, 'and then we can begin. We have so many things to go through.'

Just then the door opened and Paul strode in, followed by the jovial Frenchman, the German and behind them a young immaculate woman who Lynda deduced to be Monsieur Debray's secretary.

Paul shook hands with the men and greeted her cordially, but with a businesslike air. She thought she detected a flicker in his eye, a tiny flicker of anger or reminiscence. But it was gone as soon as it had come and she couldn't be sure. She noticed again the energy of his movement, the piercing intelligence of his eyes as he rested them on whoever came into view, the clear even tones of his voice in whatever language he used. Last night Lynda had heard him, to her amazement, speaking German with the same assurance as he handled English.

She swallowed hard and focused her mind on the business at hand. Paul was carrying a large folder—of course, the drawings and plans, she had almost forgotten them—and he placed these at the centre of the table as they all sat down.

At each seat Lynda saw there was a printed agenda and next to it a pencil and small notepad. Monsieur Debray sat at the head of the table, his secretary next to him. Stanford was at the other end and she and Paul opposite each other.

Monsieur Debray cleared his throat and began. He said, for accuracy's sake, that he would make his opening comments in French. If anyone felt he or she needed clarification, his secretary would be pleased to act as interpreter.

He then summarised the point of the meeting. They had all agreed to go ahead with two buildings in the project. The point was now to determine the size and scale of their remaining collaboration. He called on Paul to refresh their memories.

Paul spoke in French, putting the case for the full development of the project clearly and succinctly. His argument gathered in force as he passed out sheets of figures, pointing out the advantage of buying now while councils and trusts were in need of funds, before more deterioration had taken place, while employment schemes might be made use of. Then with a slight air of drama, he brought out a slide projector from his case and asked whether they would like to see the houses.

There were nods all around and the secretary rose to draw the curtains and push a button which released a large screen on to one wall.

Lynda found herself thrilling to the images. Paul had taken slides of the houses from various perspectives, and each slide of the existing house was followed on the screen by a slide of plans or occasionally a watercolour rendition of what it would be turned into.

Lynda had never seen these latter and she was amazed anew at Paul's skill and imagination. A pang of loss shot through her, but she made herself think coolly. Lucky the woman who has him, and with a wry afterthought that made her feel a little better, if she can have him to herself!

Suddenly she noticed one of her own drawings flashing on the screen and Paul explaining that the following slides showed the interiors of the first two houses. He turned the meeting over to her.

Lynda forced her voice nervously to the surface, apologised for speaking English, and then began to comment on the slides, her assurance growing as she spoke.

When the slides were finished, she asked whether the meeting would like her to comment on plans for the remaining houses. Monsieur Debray's nod gave her the cue, and remembering her discussions with Paul in almost total detail, she talked fluently about the forthcoming work. When she finished, Paul passed round photo-copies of the notes she had made, together with projected budget figures, and opened the folder of drawings for closer examination.

Amazed at her own coolness, Lynda then asked for questions. They came, fast and furious, addressed both to herself and to Paul, but she coped, adequately she felt. When there were no more, she glanced at Paul. He was smiling and gave her a long, slow wink. It gave his face a mischievous, boyish quality and she found herself disarmed, returning his smile.

Stanford then made a brief statement, saying that he, for one, was ready to support the project fully. Northrop Shaw voiced his agreement. The two Frenchmen looked at each other mutely for a moment, then Monsieur Debray, clearing his throat, said yes, he too agreed. Mr Overton and Miss Harrow had convinced him both by the thoroughness of their argument and the excellent plans. He looked at Herr Spengler and Monsieur Resnais, and they both nodded consent.

'Well, that's decided then,' said Monsieur Debray.

'It calls for a little celebration. I invite you all for an aperitif next door.'

As they left the room in single file behind him, Lynda felt her arm being squeezed and Paul's voice whispering, 'Good work, Miss Harrow!' She turned to meet his wide smile. His eyes were sparkling behind his thick lashes and he seemed to have forgotten anything that might have gone on between them the night before.

Lynda wished she could separate her personal feelings from her work with quite such ease. But as she tried to return Paul's smile openly, enthusiastically, she knew she couldn't; the very strength of his attraction made it impossible. Each of his gestures called forth another one, from another more intimate setting. She wanted to run away or run into his arms. And she could feel the smile growing false on her face.

She turned away from him to follow the others into a bright attractive room in which stood a table laden with canapés and drink. There were people she didn't recognise already in the room, drinking and talking, and she wondered who they might be.

Stanford approached her with a glass of champagne. He handed it to her and they clicked glasses.

'Congratulations. You must be a very pleased young woman,' he said.

Lynda nodded, 'I am.'

But something in the shrill pitch of her voice must have alerted him and he looked at her quizically, deeply, for a long moment. He seemed to be able to read her thoughts and she lowered her eyes.

'Still having trouble with that man?' he gestured in the general direction of Paul, who was standing by the table.

Lynda could feel the colour rising to her cheeks.

'He's an idiot. Shall I give him a talking to?'

Lynda's mouth dropped. She shook her head vigorously. 'No, it's not like that.'

'Well, what is it, then? Are you playing hard to get?'

This time she blanched, but she shook her head again.

He shrugged and then, putting his arm protectively round her shoulders, said, 'Well, if you ever want to get away from it all, just come to the United States. I wasn't joking, you know. I'll give you a job tomorrow.'

Suddenly a plan began to take shape in Lynda's mind. Yes, why not? Go to the United States, like her father. Then she could forget Paul.

'Perhaps I'll take you up on that sooner than you think,' she said to him.

He looked at her closely. 'You really mean it this time, don't you?'

She nodded, 'Yes, I think I do.'

'Well, I'll be back in my New York office on the twentieth. Just call me. I can put you up in the company apartment and we'll take it from there.' He smiled at her. 'Don't look so glum! You'll enjoy New York, you know.'

Lynda had just spotted Paul in a corner of the room on Rees's left. He was holding forth animatedly to a woman she was sure was the same as the one she had seen him with in the hotel bar. A sweeping jealousy enveloped her, made her lips tremble.

Stanford followed her gaze and then looked at her and whistled under his breath. 'You've got it bad . . .! Pull your face together and I'll bring you over to meet the enemy.'

Lynda drew back and gasped.

'Come on,' he encouraged her, 'prove your mettle.

If you can't get across the room, you'll never get across the Atlantic!'

She knew he was right and she let him take her arm and manoeuvre her across the room.

'Her name is Yvette Dorléac. She's one of Debray's crowd, has something of a reputation as a painter and is, I'm told, quite a good designer. Worthy competition.'

Lynda blanched.

'But I've never invited *her* to the States, and she's given me many an opportunity. So buck up girl.' He gave her arm a squeeze. 'And never forget you're with a very attractive man.'

She looked at him, coyly now, suddenly at her ease. 'Yes, very attractive indeed.' She said the words loudly enough for Paul, whom they were approaching, to hear. Stanford gave her a knowing smile, winked, and then turned seriously to Paul.

'I thought it might be appropriate for Yvette and Lynda to meet, given that they share interests.'

Lynda thought she could detect a momentary hesitation in Paul. But perhaps she was mistaken, for he introduced the two women with that absolute courtesy which seemed to come so naturally to him when he chose to use it.

The two girls eyed each other up and down before Yvette said, 'Ah yes, you are that miraculous young assistant Paul has been telling me so much about.' She managed to give the words a patronising edge that turned them into insult.

Lynda looked at her for a moment before responding. Then with a proprietorial air that startled her, she put her hand on Paul's shoulder. 'No more miraculous than the man I work with, I'm sure,' she answered coolly.

She could see a wide smile breaking over Rees's

face as he leapt in to fill the widening gap in the conversation. It gave Lynda a moment to glance secretly at Yvette. Damn Paul for his taste, she thought to herself. Yvette was a formidable woman.

Suddenly Lynda felt a hand on her shoulder, and turned to face Claude.

'I thought you might forget to ring me,' he said, his eyes flashing warmly in his bronzed face, 'so I came round. Can I get you a drink? Your glass is empty and these gentlemen seem busy.'

'Yes, please,' said Lynda, and turning to the little group, 'You'll excuse me for a moment . . .' She could sense Paul tensing angrily, but he said nothing.

That's that, then, Lynda thought as she followed Claude across the room. 'Goodbye, Paul Overton, goodbye to all that.'

Tears rose to her eyes, but she forced them away. A plan had begun to shape itself in her mind. She would let Claude take her sightseeing. He was heavensent as a getaway and she might as well see something more of Paris while she was here. Then she would take an early plane back to London. She couldn't face the idea of talking politely to Paul, making superficial gestures.

Claude handed her a glass of champagne.

'Shall I take you away from all these dull people?' She nodded.

'Drink up, then.'

Lynda felt a little guilty leaving without saying a word. But Stanford would understand, and luckily at the door they met Monsieur Debray, who waved off her apologies and told her to have a good time.

Claude's car stood in front of the building, a gleaming silver Porsche, its roof down, a large aerial swaying in the breeze. She noticed for the first time that he was dressed casually, in perfectly fitting jeans, blue and white checked shirt, a soft suede jacket thrown over his shoulders.

She relaxed into the car's upholstery and answered Claude's brilliant smile as he swung in beside her.

'I'll take you to a charming place I know in the Bois de Boulogne, and then we can make further plans over lunch . . .' He put a tape into the car radio and the mellow tones of a Charles Aznavour song flowed out over the street.

'I keep this for tourists,' he chuckled, giving her hand a squeeze as he manoeuvred the car outrageously through traffic.

Lynda determined to enjoy herself. Claude was pleasant enough and certainly very attractive, and she wondered a little that she didn't find herself more drawn to him. The thought brought Paul's presence dangerously close and she steeled herself to listen to Claude's explanations about the sights they were passing.

He proved to be a wonderful guide, full of anecdotes both current and historical. As her ear grew attuned to his French, she was able to catch his quick-witted asides and respond in kind, if a little slowly.

By the time they reached the restaurant, they were chatting away merrily. But the pomp of the place took Lynda's breath away: white-wigged doormen parading as eighteenth-century footmen, a gilded interior with heavy furniture and enormous mirrors. She wondered at Claude's lack of discomfort in his casual clothes.

He chuckled in her ear. 'It's for the tourists, but I enjoy it and the food isn't too bad.'

The maître d'hôtel greeted him by name and showed them to a quiet corner table which looked out on to the woods. Lynda let Claude order; a plate of charcuterie and crudités, a Châteaubriand steak with pommes dauphines and leeks for two.

'The simplest things here are what they do best,' Claude whispered to her. 'Never have their sauces.'

When the food arrived, he asked her about the outcome of the meeting.

'Good, good, then I can come to England and see you again, on your native ground,' he smiled.

Lynda's stomach tightened and she changed the subject. 'Tell me about the history of this place.'

'It used to be the summer residence of one of our estimable dukes. But then, the story goes, he squandered his money on one of the great turn-of-the-century artistes, or coquettes, I should say. The house was sold at a public auction just before his death. They say she held his hand at his deathbed, so perhaps it was all worth it for him. The moment he died, she went off with another duke, of course. Being an ageing coquette is expensive.'

Over coffee, Claude asked, 'Shall we do something silly like climbing to the top of the Tour Eiffel?'

'I didn't dare ask,' Lynda chuckled. 'I thought you'd laugh at me. But I've never been up on top.'

'Well, I haven't been for years, so let's go.'

They took the lift, then climbed the remaining stairs to the top of the tower, laughing like children, allowing themselves to be photographed by an old man who said he would send them the pictures. Claude gallantly gave the man a large tip. 'That way I sometimes get the pictures,' he whispered to her.

As they got back into the car, he turned to her, 'What shall it be next, my English Miss, country or city?'

'Give me a list of the various attractions,' she

replied, playing into his mood.

'Well—city: nightclubs, dancing, shows, dinner, the lights playing on the Seine, couples embracing in dark corners . . . Country: fast motorway, narrow lanes, villages with wonderful food, Chartres, our country house . . . Take your pick.'

'Both,' Lynda answered. 'I can't possibly decide.'

'Greedy,' he said, flashing his smile at her. 'What time do you leave tomorrow?'

'Around noon,' she lied.

'Well, if you pack your bags now, we can do both. Paris by night tonight, then a drive down to the country and the sights in the morning, if we wake early enough, that is.'

'Sounds wonderful,' said Lynda, realising that this way she could be almost certain of avoiding Paul. But suddenly she was struck by a guilty thought. If she agreed to spend the night in Claude's country house, didn't that suggest . . .

She decided to confront the issue. 'If I come with you to the house, Claude, that doesn't mean . . . I'm not committed . . . I don't want you to get the wrong impression . . .' She scrambled for words, her French failing her.

He chucked her under the chin and looked into her eyes with his satin ones, smiling, 'Don't worry, my English Miss. Don't worry. Things will take their course or they won't.' He made one of those swirling gestures with his hands which signified, 'Whatever happens will happen.' His good humour disarmed her, and she laughed, imitating his gesture.

They drove back to the hotel, joking all the way. Then Claude went to sit in a café while Lynda got her things ready. Walking through the lobby, she tried to make herself as small as possible, afraid that she might bump into Paul. She managed to get to her room without seeing him. There she threw her things into her bag and changed into her crêpe-de-chine dress. She realised as she brushed her hair that she must leave some word for Paul.

She sat down at the little secretaire to write a note, but it proved to be more difficult than she had imagined. What could she say? Finally, when all formulas failed, she decided to be honest.

'Paul,' she wrote, 'I simply can't face you . . . after all this. So I'm taking an early plane back to London.' Then, as an afterthought, she added, 'I wish I could separate my working life from my feelings as easily as you.'

She signed it, put it into a hotel envelope and made her way quietly to the lift. She left the note for Paul at reception. As she walked out of the hotel, she saw him coming up the street with Stanford Rees and Yvette. She turned in the opposite direction and fled, not stopping at Claude's café table at the corner of the street until she heard him shouting, 'Slow down. I'm right here and there's no plane to catch just yet!'

Lynda turned and slumped into a chair beside him. She was breathless, pale. She felt as if she'd narrowly escaped with her life.

Claude looked at her with concern. 'What is it, Lynda? You look as if you've just seen a ghost.'

She shrugged and tried a smile. 'I thought I'd kept you waiting far too long,' she said lamely. 'Shall we head off now?' She was afraid if they stayed here, Paul might turn up again.

Claude eyed her quizzically, but he drained his glass. They got up and walked to the car.

'I thought we might take a stroll through the Montparnasse cemetery before the light gives out,' he suggested.

Lynda voiced her approval. A cemetery, she felt, was just what she needed now to bury this part of her life.

CHAPTER TEN

It was drizzling as Lynda walked the short distance from the tube to the flat. Somehow she welcomed London's grey anonymity. It gave her space to hide, to think.

Her evening and last hours with Claude had not been a success. She had felt drained, uncommunicative, and Claude's incessant chatter had begun to grate on her nerves. He had sensed her withdrawal and, apart from a kiss, he had not pressed his attentions on her. The Debray house, Chartres cathedral, had been magnificent, but even in front of these Lynda had not been able to manifest more than a false enthusiasm. She was haunted at each turn by the decision which awaited her.

When Claude finally dropped her at the airport, she was relieved. She expressed her gratitude as best she could, apologised for her ill-humour and promised to return his hospitality if he ever came to London.

'I may just keep you to that,' he had said, and flashing the smile she had grown tired of, had walked away.

Now as Lynda climbed the stairs to the flat, she wished only for a little quiet in which to take action on the decision she had arrived at in the plane. Tricia, she prayed, would be out and she would write her letter of resignation to Mr Dunlop immediately—before she got cold feet.

But as luck would have it, Tricia was in. She got

up from the sofa the moment Lynda came through the door.

'Where on earth have you been?' she demanded.

'Paris, of course.'

'I don't understand it, then. Paul's rung from Paris continually—last night and this morning. He sounded furious, at first, anyhow. This morning he simply sounded concerned.'

Lynda blanched.

'I said I'd leave a message for him as soon as I had news of you.'

Lynda looked at her watch and then flopped on to the sofa, relieved. 'Well, he'll have left the hotel by now and he won't be back in London until much later. There's a delay at Immigration.'

Tricia looked at her questioningly, 'What's up between you two, in any case?'

Lynda tried to answer calmly, 'I'm quitting,' but the tears welled up in her eyes.

'What on earth for? You must have been doing the right thing if Paul took you along to Paris.'

'It's not that. I . . . I just can't work with him.'

'Why ever not? He's not *that* terrible, and from the look of things, I thought the two of you were getting on rather well.' Tricia gave her a sceptical glance.

Suddenly the tears poured down Lynda's face. She was sobbing, letting flow all the pent-up emotion of days.

Tricia put an arm around her. 'Tell me about it, Lynda,' she said gently, 'It might help.'

'I . . . oh, God, I'm in love with him,' Lynda stammered out between sobs.

Tricia squeezed her arm. 'I suspected as much. What about him?'

Lynda shrugged and wiped her tears with her

sleeve. 'Oh, he'd have me in bed soon enough,' she tried a watery smile. 'But there's Vanessa, and lord knows how many other women milling about.' She thought of Yvette. 'And I don't want to be part of a harem,' she brought it out with a sob. Then controlling herself, she got up to pace. She felt she had to move her limbs.

'Does he know?' Tricia asked.

Lynda looked at her aghast. 'How could he? Anyhow, it's hopeless. I'm going away. Stanford Rees has offered me a job in New York.'

'Just like that?'

'Just like that. I'm going to write a letter of resignation to Mr Dunlop now. You could bring it to him on Monday. Would you? And gather up my things for me?'

'Aren't you going to speak to Paul?'

'Oh, Tricia, I couldn't! I simply couldn't.' Lynda realised quite clearly that if Paul were to use his power over her to persuade her that professionally she had to stay put, she probably would. And then the whole miserable process would begin again.

Tricia shrugged her shoulders, 'Well, if that's the way you want it. But it doesn't seem right to me, running away like that. Think it over a little more.'

But Lynda was adamant. 'I have. I've been thinking of nothing else. It's my only hope.' She got up and walked to her room. 'I'm going to change now and write to Mr Dunlop.'

She decided to take a bath first and ponder the phrases she would use. 'For personal reasons. . . Sudden offer in the U.S. . . . Sorry, insufficient notice . . . Have terminated the first part of the project successfully. It should not be too difficult to find a replacement. . . Please convey my gratitude to Paul Overton for all the help he has given me, for all that he has taught me . . .' She was rather pleased by this last. It struck the right professional note.

She lay down on her bed to relax for a little while, but deep sleep overtook her and she woke only late the next morning. Her mind was a blank. Only the phrases of her letter to Mr Dunlop flitted in and out of it in a repetitive pattern.

She put on a pair of old jeans, made herself some coffee and sat down at the small portable typewriter to write her letter. Once it was finished she addressed it and went to give it to Tricia, who was having a late breakfast in the kitchen.

'Will you give this to Mr Dunlop first thing to-morrow?'

Tricia nodded, 'But I don't promise not to speak to Paul. After all, he's obviously been worried about you.'

'Worried about his project, not me,' Lynda said savagely. Then seeing Tricia draw back at her tone, she apologised, 'I'm sorry Tricia, I didn't mean to bark, I'm just nervous.'

The day passed uneventfully and Lynda went to bed early. She slept in a stupor and woke feeling drugged. A heaviness encased all her movements. She washed her clothes, slowly, deliberately, tidied up, then sat in a daze on the kitchen stool sipping coffee.

She had a week to waste before ringing Stanford Rees and getting a ticket, and she wasn't too sure how to spend it. Perhaps she could go home. But no, she didn't feel she could confront David either. She would write to him instead, at length.

She picked up a pencil and began doodling auto-matically on a scrap of notepaper. The telephone rang, but she didn't pick it up. Perhaps it's Paul, she thought distantly. And then what? There was not much point in talking.

She suddenly noticed that she had drawn his portrait on the scrap paper: the straight nose, strong, cleft jaw, wide cheekbones, deep-set eyes.

She went to her room to get some proper drawing paper and began to sketch again, this time more deliberately. As a child, she had learned that the best way to get something off her mind was to draw it—almost as if her fingers were engaged in an act of exorcism. And now she drew semi-consciously, drew Paul over and over, and then, before she quite realised it, her father as she remembered him in his Air Force uniform, and her mother, as an ageing woman before her death.

She did not realise that Tricia had come in until she heard her voice directly in front of her.

'Have you been sitting here all day?'

'My goodness, I had no idea it was so late!' Lynda's watch showed six o'clock.

'And you didn't answer the telephone?'

Lynda shook her head. 'It only rang once, I think . . .'

'Mr Dunlop's been trying to reach you. And Paul,' she added. Tricia looked over Lynda's shoulder at the desk. 'Good sketches. Very good. I'm sure Paul would be pleased to see them.'

Lynda shuddered and made to tear the drawings up, but Tricia stopped her. 'Don't. Leave it,' she said quietly. Then in a more official tone, 'I think you'd better come in tomorrow. There are all kinds of things to clear up—pension forms, National Insurance, not to mention some individual clients you've been handling . . .'

'How stupid of me! I'd completely forgotten. Yes, yes, of course I'll come in,' Lynda uttered. There was no avoiding it.

'Robert's coming over later. I'll cook us some dinner.'

'Wouldn't you rather I went out?' Lynda asked vaguely.

'No. It will do you good to talk, snap out of this daze.'

Lynda helped Tricia to get dinner ready and when Robert arrived, they joked and chatted casually, mostly about the U.S. and what Lynda had to prepare herself for. She excused herself early, wanting to prepare for tomorrow's office ordeal.

'See you before you go, then.' Robert gave her a brotherly kiss. 'Don't just vanish.'

She smiled and promised not to.

The next morning Lynda woke early. But she still felt dazed, her head foggy with the effort of keeping Paul out of it. Her face in the mirror looked pale and she put on some blusher. 'The point is,' she told herself over and over again, 'to look excited about going to New York.'

She felt cold and put on some wintry clothes, jeans tucked into high boots and a warm black woolly which came right up to her chin. Then she brushed her hair to a sheen. Mustn't look demoralised, she thought, and with a final gesture of self-possession, she put some shadow on her eyes and gloss on her lips.

'That's better,' said Tricia as she saw her coming into the kitchen. 'You look yourself again. You worried me yesterday.' She poured a cup of coffee for her. 'I've got to be in early today, so I'll dash. See you there. And make sure you get there,' she added in a threatening voice.

Tricia had only been gone some five minutes when the doorbell rang. Lynda went to answer, thinking

Tricia must have forgotten her keys, but the door opened on Paul. She moved instinctively to slam it again, but he was too quick for her. He caught her wrist until she released the knob and then, still gripping her wrist, slammed the door behind him. He towered over her, his eyes steely, his face slightly flushed.

'What do you mean, running out on me like that? And with that coxcomb?'

She turned her back on him, unable to meet the pressure of his eyes.

'You seemed otherwise engaged,' she shrugged. 'Happily engaged.'

He took hold of her shoulder and shook her hard.

'What kind of professional behaviour is it to walk out on Rees like that, without so much as a goodbye? How do you think I feel?'

She wriggled out of his grasp and turned on him coldly. 'I'm sorry if I embarrassed you . . . but I don't care two bits for your professionalism. And Stanford will understand.'

Paul's face looked dangerously hot now, his broad shoulders tensed beneath the leather jacket. He paced the length of the room with long strides and turned back to her.

'And what, may I ask, is the meaning of your cryptic little note? Why can't you face me? What have *I* done to *you*? I try to treat you with considera-tion on all fronts, professional and personal,' she could hear him swallow, 'help you, and what do you do? You continually walk out on work commitments, taunt me like a little vixen, only then to throw your engagement in my face. And on top of all that you run off and sleep with the boss's son!'

He was standing close to her now and before she knew what she was doing, Lynda stretched out her hand and slapped him hard, across the face. She was angry now and her words came shrilly, tumbling out one on top of the other.

'I slept with no boss's son, how dare you? And *I'm* not engaged—you never stopped to ask, just assume everything in your high and mighty fashion. *You're* the one who's attached . . . attached several times over.' She spat it out venomously. 'And I don't make a habit of casual night-time encounters with men whom I happen to work with. And I can't . . .' Her words suddenly choked as they caught a sob.

He stood there, rubbing his face where she had hit him.

Lynda ran to hide from him, her heart pounding, the tears falling furiously from her eyes. She stumbled blindly on to the sofa and flung herself down on it, hiding her streaming face in her arms.

Suddenly he was beside her, lifting her face gently away from her arms. His eyes were bright as she looked into them through her tears, the pupils darkly distinct against the blue.

'Lynda,' he murmured softly, 'what are we doing to each other?' He kissed her tears away and drew her towards him into the hollow of his arm. She snuggled against his chest, abandoning herself to the roughness of his sweater, burying her face in its warmth.

She felt she could no longer resist him. Her mind buried the Vanessas and Yvettes and countless others. Only one thought was clear to her—she couldn't do without him, and she pressed herself against him, making herself into a compact ball.

He ruffled her hair and with his hand at the back of her neck gently turned her face up to his.

'I won't let you go off to New York or anywhere. I want you here with me, working with me. I've been trying to make that clear to you and you won't listen,' he whispered, and reached for her lips with such a mixture of force and sweetness that she felt her entire body melt into the returning of his kiss. They stayed clasped together for what, to Lynda, seemed an eternity.

Then gently he released her and drew away. 'I don't want to commit the crime of a casual daytime encounter,' he said, a hint of mischief in his voice.

Lynda suddenly felt cold, abandoned, and noting it, Paul drew her to him again. 'I want you very much,' he said huskily, 'and not casually, so let's save it. Let me show you something first.' He got up and drew her after him.

Lynda looked at him questioningly, her eyes, her skin still aflame from his touch. She followed him into the kitchen, not daring to try her voice.

'Will you offer me some coffee, before we set off?'

She nodded and as she warmed it, asked, 'Where are we going?' Her voice was tremulous and he put his arm around her.

'You'll see. It's a surprise.'

Paul led her out into the brightness of the day. She felt as if she were enveloped in a dream, not daring to move too much, to speak too much, lest it should vanish. As she relaxed into the car's plush seat, she suddenly remembered, 'I promised Tricia I'd go to the office and see to things.'

'There's nothing to see to,' he said brusquely. 'You're not going away, are you?'

She looked him full in the face, met the power of his eyes and shivered. 'No, I guess not,' she said softly, and reached to touch his hand to remind herself why.

They drove without speaking through the city and then on to a country road. Paul snapped a tape into the car radio and she recognised the longing, strain-ing tones of Debussy. Little by little, the contours of the road grew familiar to her.

'I think we've been here before,' she commented.

He nodded, his eyes glowing. 'I'm very glad you remember.'

A narrow lane led them to a slope she recognised, and then a ramshackle manor house came into view.

'Why, it's your parents' house,' she said.

He chuckled as he pulled into a drive covered with weeds. 'My house now, or almost. Yours too, if you want to live here.' He stopped the car and took her hand.

'Me? With you?' She gasped the words grace-lessly.

'Well, if you'll let me into it now and then for a casual night-time encounter,' Paul laughed.

She flushed.

'Will you, Lynda? Live with me?'

'Me?' Her voice was shrill with surprise. 'But what about Vanessa? You're engaged. I thought . . .'

He cut her off abruptly, his eyes dark, 'If you're going to be my wife, you really are going to have to stop believing what you read in the gutter press. I've told you before.'

Lynda winced.

'And what *did* you think?' He was angry now and he ran a long-fingered hand abruptly through his thick hair. 'You thought I could live all these years totally celibate, never having slept with anyone, simply waiting for you to come along?' He lit a cigarette took a long puff and then crushed it brutally in the ashtray.

She looked at him, the colour warm in her face, then ran her fingers along his cheek tracing the line of his lips. 'I'm sorry,' she said softly. 'I've been an idiot.'

He caught her hand and kissed her fingertips. 'Never mind, we've got time now, day and night-time, to explain it to each other. If you'll marry such a tainted man, that is,' he added mischievously.

She breathed her yes almost inaudibly and met his lips firmly with a freshness that was full of promise.

He walked round to open her door and then taking her hand urged her into a run up to the heavily panelled front door of the house. He opened it with two large old-fashioned keys and then, as the door creaked open, Lynda found herself whisked off the ground, light as a feather in his muscular arms as he lifted her over the threshold.

'Practising for the real thing,' he drawled into her ear.

He set her down in the large wainscoted hall. They each took a breath, then made a face and burst out laughing.

'Not exactly roses, is it?' said Paul. 'But then it hasn't been lived in for a long time. We'll soon change that.'

Lynda followed him round the large well-proportioned rooms of the ground floor, then up a narrow secondary staircase which led into various levels of corridors and tiny rooms.

'It's like a maze,' she said. 'I'm quite lost.'

'That's the idea,' he grinned. 'You'll never find your way out.'

'And when I'm through with the changes, you'll never find your way in,' she parried.

He laughed and took her hand. 'It is a confusing place. It's because of all the additions made over the years. But look, come in here.'

The corridor seemed to have ended abruptly in front of a small latched door. Paul had to bend down to go in. 'My old room,' he said.

Surprisingly the small door opened on to a large attic room with sloping ceiling and windows on two sides which looked far out on to the green expanses.

'It's wonderful!' Lynda exclaimed, squeezing his hand. 'I'd love to work in here.'

'Depends what kind of work you mean,' he said, taking her into his arms and hugging her so hard she gasped.

'Not now,' she wriggled out of his arms, 'or I'll never see the rest of this house!'

A door opposite to the one they had come in by led them down three steps to what seemed a totally different house.

'The main living quarters,' Paul laughed. 'This is the newer part of the house.'

'It's enormous! What on earth shall we do with it all?' Lynda wailed as she suddenly found herself back in a room on the ground floor which she had already seen.

'It's to the drawing board for you, Miss Harrow . . . and of course, we could try filling it with a child or two.' He pulled her to him, pressing his hands to the base of her spine as he met her lips in a long kiss. Then, still holding her, he said huskily, 'Come on, there's one more thing to see.'

They walked out into unnaturally intense sunlight. Lynda blinked once or twice and then gave herself up to its brightness. Brimming over with joy, she watched Paul's lithe body through half-closed lids as he walked rapidly towards the car, opened its boot and brought out a bulky chequered blanket.

He took her hand and pulled her after him, half-running, half-stumbling down the slope through the tall grass into a copse of tall trees. Their laughter pierced the stillness.

'Welcome to my hideout,' said Paul, and led her through the dark shadows cast by the trees to a small sheltered clearing where the sun suddenly burst forth on a narrow glistening brook. Smooth pebbles shone at its base, the water rushing over them with a gentle murmuring.

Lynda stopped by its edge, letting the magic of the place penetrate her. 'It's wonderful,' she breathed. 'Not quite of this world.'

'That's what I used to pretend to myself when I was little,' he said, spreading the blanket out on the grass and drawing her down beside him.

He stroked her hair, letting his hand glide down her back, and as she thrilled to his touch, he pressed his lips to hers, urging her body to his. He searched her mouth with a burning ferocity. She could feel little flames licking her thighs, her stomach, her breasts, and she clung to him, letting her hands explore the tautness she had been so afraid of.

Paul pulled her up on him and raised her face above his, smoothing her cheeks, her lips, with the roughness of his fingers. Then he pulled the chain around her neck out on to her sweater.

'The ring's gone.' He looked at her questioningly. Then abruptly, 'So I was right—there was someone. When did you take it off? Who is he?' His brow furrowed as his eyes grew black with anger.

Lynda was dismayed by the barrage of questions, the sudden shift of mood. 'An old friend, a childhood friend. We thought that perhaps . . . but it was only friendship.'

He sat bolt upright and took her roughly by the shoulders. 'Don't lie to me, Lynda Harrow!'

She moved out of his grasp, angry herself now.

'I'm not lying! I don't lie. And stop bullying me, you ... you insufferable bully!' She stood up and began to walk away, the tears coming to her eyes with the hopelessness of it all. He caught her by the ankle and taking her hand pulled her down beside him.

'I'm sorry,' he stroked her hair again, whispering. 'I'm sorry, I just can't bear to share you with anyone, not even a memory. And I always seem to see you in the arms of other men. It's a little daunting.'

'Me?' She looked at him aghast.

'Yes, you, Lynda Harrow,' he said her name again in that particular way which had so discomfited her. 'In pubs, on dance floors, at dinners, in lifts— Robert, Rees, that French coxcomb—the list seems endless.'

Lynda laughed. 'I was just trying to run away from you and your Vanessas and Yvettes!' She looked at him tauntingly now, from beneath her dark lashes. 'When did you first notice me, then?'

'Oh, I don't know,' he met her tone, 'in the bath, I guess.'

The colour rose to her face and she lifted an arm to slap him, but he caught it and laughed. 'I noticed you from the first, Lynda Harrow. In Mr Dunlop's office, the day of that initial meeting. I said to myself: "That one, that one will be off with a man before the project's half under way." That's why I was so against it. And I was right, wasn't I?' He put his arm around her. 'I just got the man a little mixed up.'

She smiled at him. 'I was terrified of you.'

'And so you should be,' he glowered at her, and then broke into a laugh. 'But you have a funny way of showing it ... Throwing clothes in my face, seducing our top client—well, in a manner of speaking,' he corrected as she gave him a black look, 'threatening to quit time and again. But it was the clothes that did it. When you threw them at me, I knew I'd had it. I was hooked. But I thought you'd still succumb to my charms in a less complicated manner,' he chuckled.

Lynda's face fell. 'If you don't want me to stay . . .'

He drew her to him, 'I'm just teasing. I want you very much. Too much.' His mouth pressed down on hers, imprinting his words on her lips and she opened to him, moaning softly as his body touched hers. He pulled the blanket round them and as he bared her skin to kiss her throat, her breasts, she could feel his urgency mingled with a new tenderness. Her skin thrilled to his touch, every pore alive to his caress, and she returned them now, heedlessly, letting his rhythm become hers. Through the throbbing of her pulse she heard a whisper in her ear—perhaps it was the rippling of the brook. 'Trust me, Lynda. Trust me.'

And as she opened her eyes to see his blue ones glowing on her, she caught herself saying with a surprising sureness, 'I do.'

News about your favourite novels

Send us your name
and address on a postcard
and we'll send you full details
about our forthcoming books.

Send your postcard to:
Mills & Boon Reader Service, Dept H,
P.O. Box 236,
Thornton Road,
Croydon, Surrey
CR9 3RU, England.

Or, if you live in North America, to:
Harlequin Reader Service, Dept. M.B.,
Box 707, Niagara Falls, N.Y. 14302

Here is a selection of Mills & Boon novels to be published at about the same time as the book you are reading.

MIXED FEELINGS	*Kerry Allyne*
INVISIBLE WIFE	*Jane Arbor*
SPITFIRE	*Lindsay Armstrong*
EGYPTIAN HONEYMOON	*Elizabeth Ashton*
RENDEZVOUS WITH A DREAM	*Margaret Baumann*
EMERALD CAVE	*Gloria Bevan*
THE SAVAGE TOUCH	*Helen Bianchin*
ANOTHER TIME, ANOTHER PLACE	*Katrina Britt*
ANOTHER LIFE	*Rosemary Carter*
SHADOWED REUNION	*Lillian Cheatham*
DARK REMEMBRANCE	*Daphne Clair*
LOVE AT SECOND SIGHT	*Kay Clifford*
THE SISTER AND THE SURGEON	*Lynne Collins*
WITCHING HOUR	*Sara Craven*
ONE OF THE BOYS	*Janet Dailey*
FLASH POINT	*Jane Donnelly*
THE STORMS OF SPRING	*Sandra Field*
MAJOR MIKE	*Hazel Fisher*
ALWAYS THE BOSS	*Victoria Gordon*
ARCTIC ENEMY	*Linda Harrel*
THE DRIFTWOOD BEACH	*Samantha Harvey*
COPPERS GIRL	*Rosalie Henaghan*
FALCON'S PREY	*Penny Jordan*
PASSIONATE STRANGER	*Flora Kidd*
UNTAMED WITCH	*Patricia Lake*
DANGEROUS	*Charlotte Lamb*
ILLUSION	*Charlotte Lamb*
DREAM ISLAND	*Roumelia Lane*
CONFIRMED BACHELOR	*Roberta Leigh*

£4.55 net each